The

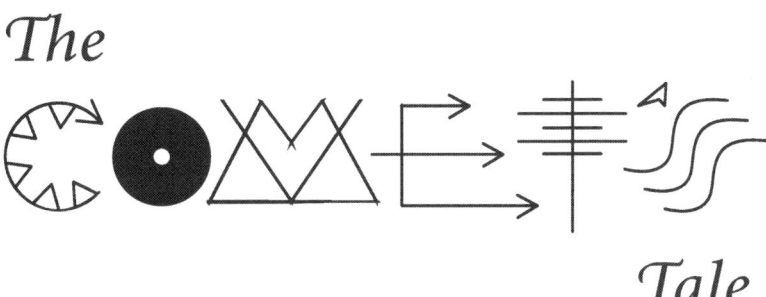

Tale

by Paul Seftel

"*He who travels far will often see things far removed from what he believed was Truth. When he talks about it in the fields at home, he is often accused of lying, for the obdurate will not believe what they do not see and distinctly feel. Inexperience, I believe, will give little credence to my song.*"

~ Ancient words of an unknown mariner.

For my family and friends along the way.

A Comet has Two Tales;
One of Dust and One of Vapor.

Contents

1. Tantric Dreams

Piercing light cracked the egg from the inside out. The End of Time, this was the beginning of the Dream. Twenty-one young, I was just a fool getting to know myself—getting to know the universe and myself. Initiate in nature's esoteric school of self-realization, my idea of good higher education was to be all about experience. I'd arrived at my cusp, the edge of a huge precipice within. A stomach full of butterflies and mind full of Déjà vu, I had to make the crossing.

Heat lightning cracked in the tropic night and the cloves smoked through the electric air. A foot taller than everyone around, my shaven head and tall pale ass was in a place more foreign than I could've imagined. A land of active volcanoes and fertile landscapes electrified by lightning storms, ancient etiquettes and komodo dragons were all incomprehensible to me. I thought I was ready for a whole new horizon in the mystic Far East but I was falling into an abyss. Summer of '95 and I stayed in Jakarta that first night, looking around the little ramshackle hostel lodging in the early morning light, open sewer watercourses and mosquitos, I figured I was ready to head out across the land. Catching a bus to a beach town on the southern ocean, the black volcanic sand met the yellow sandstone cliffs. Déjà vu. Hewn into the rock faces way up high, the caves accessible only by rope ladder intrigued me. Happily I found a clean and comfy inexpensive place to stay close to the ground, in one of the many hotels along the beach. Déjà vu.

I took a walk down the road checking out stalls of artist's crafts and batik painting. I met an artist whose work I really liked—her midnight blues, astral fires and faces cut with fiery marks into the batik linen. I dug it so I bought it and she invited me in for a bite, knowing I was hungry. Enjoying her hospitality and the view from her wood shack, we talked about art, painting and the spirits of the South Seas depicted in so many of the works of art, paintings and carvings of wood and stone. She made me a delicious mushroom omelet and sat with me whilst I ate, saying she weren't hungry. Something was a little strange and I did wonder, and then it dawned, the way I was asked if I'd like mushrooms… and it was too late. Roost to table, I'd devoured it wolf like. Though I did wonder.

It was sunset and I headed towards the beach and the Temple of Ancient Kings I'd seen on the map in my guide book. The sun was setting, silver sky soft pink with luminous blue hues. The temple was surreal, many columned above a checkered paved ground, no roof but the shifting colors of the sky. There were a few locals and visitors walking around and it seemed like you could climb, touch and sit anywhere, everything sacred, nothing roped off in this old ruin by the beach. The whole place beaming, radiating power, I sat on the meditation and initiation stone. At the heart of the roofless many columned temple, the geometry began to shift. The columns became liquid light, rippling with forms, reflecting the sunset night. The mushrooms were starting to kick in and I became self-conscious in the temple hot seat under the wonder dome. Aware of watching eyes, other figures, people and shadows shuffled around. Shadows approaching, wanting to guide, befriend, rob me, it was hard to tell. Shaking them off, I walked down to the ocean's edge and sat cross legged on the black sand watching the fiery pink sunset turn to red blue purple blackness. The emerald green woolen hooded sweatshirt I wore felt like it was aglow with a magical light, like a dim firefly; I thought only I might be seeing it.

Sitting there—looking into the darkness, an all-consuming hole appeared to open sesame in the ocean like a warm envelope. In the heart of darkness where above and below meet, the electric shimmering heat hazed the Southern Ocean, Ratu Kidal the Goddess Spirit of the South Seas emerged on wings of astral fire. Lucid and wide eyed, vision ablaze in the darkness, she appeared from the ocean distance. Melting into her, this ecstatic prismatic light, astral reality as all is, an incredible warm glow overcame me from the crown of my head down and back up again like a writhing beam of serpentine light.

In the next swelling moment I felt an elephant's trunk emerge from my face, a surreal plasma body being drawn in waves of light. My belly bloomed round and full, relaxing cross legged in the lotus position, root firmly planted in the ground. Time passed, like a sitcom on the sofa, I whisked off into stories of myself through time. And time again. Back in my full senses again, body and mind on the black volcanic sand, I was no doubt at the far out edge of the world.

Picking up and walking down the beach, I remembered I was in Java. Java! I knew not where I was. I had zero point of reference based on experience, even an abstract notion of place, in being there. So far away in my own dimension, dissolving and forming. Atomic zero. I felt pretty alone and creepy in the misty ocean darkness, seeing groups of people leaping and dancing round fires. When I did remember the name of my lodgings, of course there where a dozen places all with that same name. The cosmos giggled. There's only one name, but many versions to reality. At least half a dozen places shared the name and I kept asking myself "where do we come from?!" Pretty sober by now, lucid, it felt really late when I did finally get back to my hotel, but I quickly discovered that only a few hours had passed. Time had warped, new worlds encountered, still only a few twilight hours clicked on.

I was glad I bought the painting. I unrolled it and tacked it up on the wall seeing that I had stepped into that prismatic electric sea of faces looming through the blue black purple mist. Quite a trip!

Chatting with the hotel owner for a while having drinks at the bar, he shared all sorts about the place and his own world travel experiences and the early Indonesian aboriginals. He brought out a short branch of a eucalyptus tree that been eaten through by termites—a small didgeridoo—to take out to the beach and play. On the black sand with the bright moon illuminating crashing waves, I found for the first time my breath able to circulate within the wood, a primal, resonant sound formed to carry my breath in a deep hum, the source of sound and vibration moving through, heart and mind combined. Wide shut, when I did open my eyes to stare into the dark horizon, the Goddess of the night and stars above, I could see constellations and twinkling stars lining up. I saw how the ancients used them as the foundations of time, navigated ocean paths, joining the dots through winding change. And I heard a small voice within.

You leave on the same star upon which you arrive

That's what a tribe called the Kogi believed. They lived in a pyramid mountain in Peru and called themselves humanity's Elder Brother. Believing the universe was a map, a mirror, and a holographic reflection, that when it saw itself, wormholes could open for the ascended spirits and celestial bodies to return on their passage through space time.

I stayed there on the beach by the South Seas another couple of nights, chilling, reaching inwards, getting acclimatized. Watching, mesmerized by the heat haze, lightning storms shifted with the clouds over the dark ocean. Sitting, walking and contemplating the dense sensation of ocean air and electric primal volcanic heat, the whole soup stewed within me as I looked into my cards, considering my next step.

Incurably fascinated with mysterious things, I was compelled by the idea that there could be secrets long hidden from the eyes of the world—mystic teachings available to everyone who sought them. There had to be greater truths—an objective truth that people shared in the world as opposed to lies and half-truth that controlled the populace. I wasn't buying it. And it was worth investigating. Shrouded in myth and confusion, hidden from inquisitors for many centuries, it had to be deciphered. Truth was separate and veiled. Worlds existed beyond my comprehension, thrusting me into the supernatural. I knew there was something out there, elusive, personal, spiritual, mystical as it was and would be to uncover.

Millennial fever was spreading hope and anticipation, the warning signs and prophecies of time sweeping away the collective mind. Love and energy combined, this was where true magic existed. The kind of magic and light that lifted us closer to what we had all known back in the dawn days, when we built our lives out of the dirt and gave thanks to Sky and Earth for dear life. Change and return, we knew we were connected to one another as to the stars and planets, long haul voyaging through space time. Astronomers looked through giant mirrors, seeing the legions of comets that swam beyond the dark edge of Jupiter, awaiting the stage in the celestial symphony.

Comets were messengers, imbued with hidden powers and unknown origins, mysteries and histories, the universal poetics and elemental integration at their core. Unpredictable in nature, teaching time travelers from the ancient of days, some enlightened ones had come at the dawn of it all, others had been here since. Many would awaken anew through a close encounter with our planetary star, like fresh batches of enlightened eggs hatched from the cosmic roost. Slowly surely, something 'other'— something beyond 'self', infected consciousness. Modern culture, society and thought awakened for mysteries of life and lives through time to be revealed. Whole constellations of stars gathered, magnetizing particles of forgotten dust. Though the spirits of the ancestors, suppressed voices, promises and memories still haunted, crying out in the deep echoing pockets of space.

The black volcanic matter opened its raw nature, the seething tropical wound and scar of primordial earth revealed. Transfixed by ideas of finding and following signs and omens, was it all to be a self-fulfilling prophecy? Was there something out there for me to find? How far did I have to go to see that thing within me? I had so many questions, and more than the answers, I was looking for the right questions. I'd silently ask these things all the time, trying to unravel the conundrum that I am. I'd ask myself to wake up, wake up to a bigger picture at hand, because I knew I was sleeping compared to what I might otherwise know or realize. Spiritual warrior in training, I was looking for a teacher of sorts. Yoda had made a profound impact on my early consciousness and

I was feeling the force in my own cosmic opera. Flying to the other side of the world, I surely felt I'd arrived on another planet.

As a teenager, camped out at a mates' place after partying in the fields on the edge of London, I'd dreamt of Java. Late night, drunk, sixteen, crashing out in the same room we'd each have crazy dreams and visions. Happy to share the stories and dream worlds on waking, sometimes we'd even find we were in the same place and we'd remember some of the things we saw together. One of those nights I first went to Java. Java! I'd never heard of the place, perhaps I'd seen it in the newspapers, though I didn't really know. This was different, cinematic, like nothing I could remember. Very fiery was the dream, it seemed as though I had won an assignment as a photojournalist, and I just couldn't turn it down. It felt like an honor; an important opportunity, but it also felt like I was burning and falling, lucidly falling, and falling, into fields of fire.

The dreams' liquid nature haunted me for years. Not knowing what had happened in Java through the previous decades, as it hadn't been reported much on western news media, I later discovered there'd been a huge massacre of artists, writers, intellectuals and students, like had gone on in other places too, who'd been disappeared for being outspoken against capitalism in its sweeping development of Jakarta.

Remaining present, neither past nor future, Java began looming in my consciousness in the early 90^s. Seeing the four letter word everywhere I began to take it as a sign or omen. It might have been the birth of the new programming language—or the beginning of the coffee boom that had slunk its way into my head, but looking deeper I realized that it was a rare gem I was looking for. The place where the world's mystics of all faiths, backgrounds and religion had been inspired by something deeper.

From that first Java dream and maybe way before, persistent omens beckoned me, offering strange grants of understanding. As I got closer I felt the grip, its gravity pulling as I reckoned I had nothing to lose, as I hurtled towards a black hole of personal oblivion, tripping up over my own feet through an ancient revered land.

Too close to see the forest for the trees, my whole phrasing of the question was turned inside out. I'd ask does lightning know itself? What is the fire saying? But like lightning and fire nothing could stop my inquisitive spirit, hungry for answers of the time in which we lived.

I'd been told about a spot in Solo—Surakarta that intrigued me. There was a special place with a three-thousand year old well, and a master who preferred to be called a Gatekeeper. I heard he offered visitors daily meditation practice. Definitely odd to travel to the other side of the planet just to sit still for a while, but I had a long way to go, to travel far to find something close to home.

A 'being' meditation. I didn't know what that really meant. I liked that. It sounded simple enough, and I knew secrets and magic were infused in the Javanese culture. Keen to go deeper and see what would be divulged, I was looking for answers. I had a lot of questions, essentially impossible questions—whys, whats and hows. I was so sensitive and intuitive in otherworldly ways to which there was no road map, falling into the mystic, wondering where I'd come out the other side.

Twenty-one young and out on my own pontoon, pushing my luck in a fated game. The air was thick, throbbing, and I was a lightning rod charged with conducting my way through. Testing the boundaries of spirit, seeing through the veils of reality into otherworldly possibility, I had no idea where I was, what I was doing, and that spirituality could indeed be so powerful. Young fool, I simply didn't know my ass from a hole in the ground.

"Simplest philosophy in the universe, one letter, just B."

The eighty-eight year old Gatekeeper, sweet and serious in temperament would repeat, his golden white hair growing in dark at the roots.

"Are you a human being or a human doing?" He'd ask within the surrealist dream, this living theatre. Intimate as a white marble temple room could be, giant crystals and a seated golden Buddha, never more than a dozen or so visitors and guests sat comfortably upright in chairs, shoes off and feet planted on the floor, making sure every toe touched ground.

The Gatekeeper sat in the chair with the crystal perched on a small shelf above and began channeling the meditation. Starting with the toes and the warm glow of relaxation, letting go, the energy began to rise up through our feet, heels, ankles, calves, slowly surely, these magical internal fires allowed each of the muscles and joints to experience a loving infusion, a cellular reboot. The soft spoken guidance carried us away within, transiting bodies and mind in this, the center of being.

In small bubbling circles the chi fires sparked from the base, the red root, seat of the serpent, circuit board of the spine. Eyes closed, internal fires bright, inner radiances and sensations rose in colored spheres of energetic light. Tuning in for daily Technicolor visions, I became more crisply attentive to thoughts, feelings, movements and actions. Light and grace becoming apparent in all, these meditative sessions were very intimate, personal and cosmic, our collective participation often boosted one another like a secret bank of batteries powering up something far greater, finding our own highest function along the way.

A gal named Maya was staying there. Ten years or so older than me, she was in her mid-thirties. Energetically and physically there was an electric spark between us, a very powerful attraction and magic. I liked older women. She was a dancer, staying in Java studying the movement arts along-side her daily meditation practice. In the thrust of so much dance and introspection she had chosen to remain silent for ten days to explore her sense perceptions and flowing waters even deeper. The silence an aphrodisiac, swiftly we hit it off—the sweetness of her fire simply electrifying. A white streak through her dark hair framed her deep brown eyes, Maya's witchy woman darkness streaked through her bright soul, her seductive power keeping us in a constant state of play. Between meditation and sleep we found an intense chemistry, the serpent kundalini fire rising within, momentum building in small circles.

Sweet and soulful, our intimacy was a complete breakdown—a dissolution of oneself and one another. Glimpsing a universal, pure form of love, we basked in the bliss of hummingbirds and flowers. Beyond who we were, lifetimes of experience and emotion moved through us like wind in sails and meteors in the sky. For hours on end—four to six hours at a time we'd make love every day for weeks.

I was so naturally high I was floating, until I began to stumble. In the tantric dance of ecstatic meditation we reached upwards into a kind of Samadhi, enlightenment and bliss. I felt and saw myself pop out of the top of my head, seven of me appearing all lined up in a row. In the beautiful entanglement, emotion swung to every place of power and opposition whilst writhing in our shared magic. Like comets crossing paths in a close encounter, the light flared all around us. At one point both of our eyes changed color, awash in the astral wake, spiraling from dark brown through green to blue. My body filled with light, feeling almost superhuman, invincible, floating. Even gravity was intoxicatingly different, my particles working in waves I hadn't felt before.

As the days flew by, I started questioning. Whos, whats and whys. Vexing unnecessary mental muscles, trying to dissect the moment and watch it crack into its knowable parts. It was like the alabaster egg I'd been given as a small boy that I had to crack open, see what was inside and watch that smooth rounded whole light all turn to dust,

I wondered who she was and what was this energy overcoming me and her and us? Was there an elephant in the room? Who was this Goddess?

The tantric energy, the fiery steed I was riding started to lash, quickly becoming a darker force. The sky and earth reaching deep into the underworld, Kali came, her inner destroyer riding me under her way like a fierce and mighty bird, taking me in, willing to consume life unto death. Brought to my most animal survival instinct— beyond awareness, I came, arriving and leaving in the same moment, exploding body and mind into ten thousand tiny particles.

You arrive on the same star on which you leave.

Everything changed. Thrown back off the bed and onto the floor by the side, I felt green with sickness. I saw the force making its way from the light worlds and choosing that moment of conception as life. I remembered choosing my own life, being in that school of light where we'd go learn about ourselves between worlds. It was there I saw the vision of another watching me with loving and protective eyes. I remembered and felt all my silent hopes, dreams, choices, and purpose, and tasted it all in that one moment. Swallowed and consumed my stomach stayed in my mouth overwhelmed by the completeness of my own disintegration.

II. Darkness falls ~ Light floats

Why did the chicken cross the road?
To get to the 'other' side.

As night turned to light, unsure which way to turn I decided to make a pilgrimage—go on an adventure and visit a volcano I'd heard about. A sacred place that was considered a gateway to the source, Mount Bromo. It was a good distance from Solo, and to get there I sat in buses and shared taxis for a day into night. Between sleep and awake I dreamt of strange ceremonies and encounters with Hindu spirits. Before waking, I was in a house in Scotland by the sea with a girlfriend from years earlier, when Ganesh the elephant deity stormed in and blew me away with a shotgun.

Shaken into waking life, stunned, I came around in the taxi ride, the car pulled up and the driver pointed to a trail he said went to Mount Bromo. Headed for sunrise and pointed into the deep purple blackness, crossing the road, I walked off into the dark.

The moon had descended, and I was alone in the dust with just starlight and shadow. In the sand sea desert, micro breezes and sand made dust devils that danced and skirted all around me. It was a long walk in the dark at 2 am, solitary but not alone and I was a bit spooked I must confess. This was real spirit land and I was really seeing things.

I had been taking this one malaria pill called Larium. It was the drug recommended as the best anti-malarial course, and it seemed like a smart move at that time. Very few side effects were disclosed and my dosage was once a week, but it was recommended to begin the preventive course a little while before the trip. I saw later how chemically adjusted I'd been by this powerful drug, contributing to the visions of the other world that step by step I had swiftly fallen into, way deeper than I knew.

The constant sense of Déjà vu, that lucid, more than a dream feeling intensified and characterized my experience. Little did I know, the psychological effects of Larium—its chemical name mefloquine—included hallucinations, visions, depression, dizziness, fatigue, loss of balance, suicidal tendencies—amongst other things— and these disconcerting symptoms and states could occur for weeks, months, years or just remain permanently. The drug had been created for and used in the Vietnam War, to devastating effect, its doses later altered for the peace corps and prescription, side effects undisclosed. Young travelers like me and my friends through the '90s and for years to come had been given the drug, sensitive souls affected by this powerful chemical.

No stranger to traveling or being on my own, this time round I was disconcertingly uncomfortable in my skin, feeling the burn of my inner fires in this alien land. My flashlight worked but at times I switched it off, wanting my sight to better adjust. I must've walked for a good hour before I saw torches way off in the distance—another path, well travelled, unlike the one I was on. I kept on walking, hoping, assuming, trusting paths would meet. And then I came upon the shadow of a building. Surprising as it was to see a grand structure looming out there in the desolate desert plain, the bulbous blue blackness of a Hindu temple loomed against the indigo sky. I thought I must be on the path.

Torch off, I kept walking. And then I knew I had lost the way. I must've been on the backside of the building, poorly navigating a way through desert brush in the red purple darkness. My torch wasn't very bright and neither was I, being out there on my own in the dark, looking for answers from a volcano at sunrise. What in the name of the cosmos was I hoping to find?! In every step the feeling of dissolution quickly grew within me. And then it was gone. Gone. The ground was gone. Pulled away like a rug underfoot, in the deep purple chasm I was falling, falling, falling. Puckered wide open. Yet somehow still. A strange gravity was at work now and I knew, just knew, I was done. Falling in the abyss, pitch darkness, time stalled and I swiftly became light. Whisked up. Light as a feather in ways words could never describe. White Light. Pure. Joy.

Bliss. No Fear. Too late for fear. Free, I thought. Golden white light surrounded me like a cloud, enfolding my outstretched body in astral fire. The lightest light, flowing deep peace, in the waters of beyond. Beyond waking life. Free at last. Free falling.

Over the edge, the ground had disappeared. Into a black hole I had stepped through a wormhole between Earth and Sky. The sensation of floating was deceptive, fooling even the winds. In total stillness the ground rose up to meet me, and like lightning I struck the Earth. Where the hard wet sand ended and I began was hard to decipher. A feather turned to stone. The flight was fossilized, impact swallowing me whole. I had seen myself falling many times—childhood nightmares recurring somewhere between dreaming and being awake. I had seen my impact, leaving my body and observing myself from above as I floated through the air. Always falling into my own intense fear, encircled by an epiphany as I plummeted towards my oblivion. So many repetitive childhood nightmares and now real, I was falling through all of them, waking into a reality of the dream.

Somewhere in the darkness of the chasm that towered above me in its stark and violent violet specter, the space between me and the Earth was definitely intimate. We had merged, I'd fallen into her scar, her root, her channel. Stumbling over myself into her underworld. I suspected I'd come to Java to face my deepest fears—to be initiated in the secrets, mysteries, teachings that came from beyond. Heaven's door had been knocked and she had answered, taking me in the ancient temple, bringing me into her sacred library, sharing the intimacy of the inner sanctum.

Being there, I had known nothing and I began to see and find more than I could ever have imagined. From the black sands of that southern ocean where I heard her call, I had glimpsed a world beyond, having shadows of memories, remembering the stories told of the ancient ones, the supernatural teachers. The masters who had once lived in those caves, Guardians of the teachings of the Goddess. It too was true that her dark ways scared most seekers away and those who sought to really know—those who submitted themselves to her great passion—had all chosen a sacred and powerful personal ultimatum.

The great sacrifice could never be compared, and for those who know not what they do, she would gladly steal that rare lamb into her dominion, devouring truth with love and love with truth until all was stripped away. Raw and revealing, painful as it was true, she had cast me under her spell, pulling me into her cave of secrets, sharing her ocean bed. Her every touch had been fire, burning passion disintegrating in its own heat 'til there was nothing left of me. Flayed, flesh pulled from bone, heart from mind, body from soul, tethered and tattered on the ocean bed in ancient desert, unattached to time, space or form. Pulled apart, untangled, friends, family, ambition and desire had melted away. All I could see was a white light piercing my mind like the sun, a golden crescent of diamonds squeezing my brain.

As the light dimmed to a slow flash, I began to hear my breath. Inhaling deeply through my nostrils I could taste the sand and salt on my lips. Red, green and blue, dark hues flashed before my eyes in the spectral blackness. The humid earth kissed my cheek giving me little idea how long I'd been unconscious. I was at the bottom of a deep pit… deep in it. Looking up, I had fallen a long way— maybe 80 feet onto hard wet sand, a ravine of a desert river bed.

"Wake up!" I heard my own voice inside. Coming to, stars all around, my particles circled and coalesced back into me, wondering whether to return to their points of light in the sky or back into my body. Molecules abuzz, they looked for the place they came from. Body cold and damp, limbs numb, my body felt like a giant bruise as I rolled onto my back and lay there looking up, and at my hand which felt surely mangled. My right hand. It had touched the ground first, just a fraction further in its outreaching flight. First touch had pushed the middle finger back, knuckle dislocated awkwardly into my palm. Body throbbing, every part of me heavy and light, the cat bounce of the fall had me curled up in a ball, waiting for some magical balloon to come and lift me up and sweep me away.

At the bottom of the ravine I struggled onto my feet, footing not so sure, balancing my way against the rock face down which I'd just fallen, steadying my way across the hard wet riverbed. I followed it back and up onto a ledge which led the way to a chimney like rock opening. Stepping up, feeling my muscles and bones like lead, I felt so heavy, all the weight of the throw down. The ledge further deceived my eyes. Thinking it was solid it became liquid—a film of sand disguising a large water filled rock pool, slipping my step and giving me a quick douse before I pulled myself out. Rolling over again, swallowed up by the Earth, I just lay put, giddy on a rock watching the stars disappear, darkness shifting frame by frame for hours. In the green of first light I saw the watchers eyes again staring down at me, a ray from beyond what I had forgotten.

Looking into them, they burned through me. The planets, stars and moving points of light disintegrated into the limitless morning sky. Raising myself when there was ample light and fewer shadows to play with my mind, my hand throbbed. Starting to swell, I was not so well. All manner of endorphins had kicked with the hit, battling to fight the pain. Working hard within, grit in my teeth from eating the dirt, breath like fire, the giddy agony moved through me and I drank it all in like some euphoric cocktail. Running like a stampede of horses through my head were thoughts of how I was going to heal myself, my all-important right hand. Out there, really out there, I thought the best way was likely ahead than back, at least to Bromo where I knew there'd be visitors for sunrise.

Finding my way clearly now, I knew I wasn't far and started to hear voices in the distance. Gathered around the base of Bromo's cinder cone were vendors serving tea and coffee brewed over small fires in the crisp dawn. I was cold. I'd been at the bottom of a hard wet pit for a few hours, and every part of me ached and stung, hammered on the anvil of Earth. I sat with one of the vendors by his fire and warmed my bones a bit. Seeing my hand and me all out of sorts, he took hold of it and tried to massage the dislocated knuckle back into place but it was already a swollen lump of meat. Why hadn't I tried to reset in out there in the night? Yank it back into its spot? Would've hurt like hell and I was barely conscious—not really in my right mind. As I lay there, I just kept thinking 'I must learn to heal myself.'

I needed to get back to Solo where my belongings were and I could get to hospital and sort myself out. Any which way it was a journey to the bus station and then a long bus ride, as had been the previous days adventure in getting there, and now I was heading back, making the same route as I had planned. It was just the fall that wasn't planned. By me at least. I had kept my spirit guides quite busy.

Seeing that I was at the volcano I thought I should walk her rim and see into her core like I'd gone there for. Looking into her, I knew I'd stepped over the edge of my life in every way. Still so jittery as I was, I walked that thin lipped rim with one dodgy hand, beat up bod and messed up balance writhing within.

The morning was heating up; I just had my t shirt on my back, cargo pants and green hoodie tied around my waist, my swollen hand on my left shoulder, swelling up like a melon in a baseball mitt. I caught up with a few other travelers who were walking west to the villages where we could get to the bus station. We walked a ways, a good couple of hours through the sand sea desert around the base of the accordion rutted volcanic mouths until we got to the mountain road and the shade of the trees. Then we walked another long way, up and down the dirt track taking another hour or so, 'til we reached a small village. Climbing into the back of a big open truck with other locals, we rode for another hour into the main town, where I could catch a bus back to Solo.

A feverish way, the dark night had met up with itself in the long day. Mad dog and Englishman. Bouncing down the rocky road in the back of that truck with locals and travelers, I kept my hand hidden under my shirt, trying to maintain breath and composure with my pain, an inner test compounded by the tight heave of bodies in the back there with me.

Reaching the bus station, I sat and waited. The next scheduled bus was 11pm and that was 8 hours away. I was in no mood for moving around, all I could do was sit there and feel it out, trying to control the pain misfiring the circuit boards inside me, and trying not to pass out. My acute awareness of these subtle movements of energy through my body had all been activated; all cylinders were firing. And with this beat of internal rhythm were light filled visions, color painting my emotional fields in liquid light. Re-attuned through Maya's intimate teachings and the Gatekeeper's guidance, it had been a complete reprogramming of sorts and I was more aware than ever before of the delicate balance of human nature, our mutual blend of left and right, dark and light.

Female and male, receptive and creative, yin and yang, this free flowing ball of energy had spun out of control. Moving through my body and cycling back around, my mind, heart and muscles behind my eyes throbbed intensely. Sitting on the bus all night long, traveling through the Javanese landscape of lightning forks and clouds of clove, the follicles of my shaven hair were already so raised that the reckless driving of the bus into oncoming traffic no longer phased me. I just sat there with my endorphin cocktail, exhausted dreaming and half visions in the red night 'til the dawn. At last back in Solo, I crashed hard on my bed for a few hours.

Flipped back in a claw like fuck me, I hoped I could somehow swiftly and simply relocate my dislocated middle finger and knuckle. Referred a doctor at the local hospital to go see, the hospital seemed pretty basic and the doctor frankly scared me. He was creepy eerie but in deep waters I entrusted myself to his expertise, for what else was I to do? Told that no surgery was necessary, I was back twenty-four hours later for them to perform the relocation with a general anesthetic, and counting backwards I was being put to sleep. Pretty damn scary, going under in Java not knowing what or where, but at least a couple of people knew I was there and would hopefully be able to account for body snatching that I might unwittingly be party to. But what was left for me to fear? Hadn't I just died?!? I'd already stepped beyond, out of body, left the building so completely.

Another layer of the onion being peeled back, raw and revealing, it forced me into a further complete letting go. When I eventually came round again, waking from the chemically induced sleep, I saw red. More than the light coming through my eyelids whilst I was under, I felt so much anger it was intense. Surprised to be back in my body, yet again, I felt sucker punched. I don't think I wanted to come round. That space I had hit in the fall, that intoxicating Elysium, that's where I wanted to be, and I was angry at my mortal coil that had brought me round.

My hand wrapped in a bandage, it throbbed and hurt like hell. Laying there for a good long while grinding my teeth and fuming, the nurse finally came and sat me up, giving me a painkiller and some scripts for more meds before bidding me on my way. Swept with fire, I tried to keep it cool with more meditation. Looking for the deep chill, mind body awareness could perhaps cool my jets and directly affect my physical being.

A couple of days had now passed since I ate dirt in that big hole. Under a lucid spell, that night after the morning's hospital excursion I took off the bandage, seething as the pain seared me rare and bare. I needed to see what they'd gone and done to better it. Not a fan of meds, I hadn't filled any of the scripts so there was no masking the pain and it simply didn't feel right.

Removing the crepe bandage, there was a rock in my palm and a blister pushing on the knuckle that was still, to my dismay dislocated. They'd knocked me out, yanked my finger, shoved a rock in my hand and strapped it up. But it wasn't working. The tendon had wrapped its way around the joint, not letting go, holding it back from finding its natural place.

I don't know how or why I remained so calm and collected. My dear fucked up right hand met with healers there in Java for the next three days who all patiently tried to relocate the finger and knuckle using all manner of weight and counterbalance release techniques. But the swelling and the tendon were not permitting, the natural law not allowing and it was getting close, close to a shitty ticket between luck and fate.

One handed in Java was not against all odds, but proved to be a great challenge. In the land of ancient etiquette and limited paper products, toilet habits were conducted with the left hand and the eating and shaking of hands done with the right. Even buttoning my trousers one handed was awkward.

Maya was amazing, taking care of me sweetly and helping me not be too clumsy. But it felt very different between us. A spell had been broken, I was shattered within, and she was now speaking. We found a completely different rhythm as friends and I was thankful for her. But also I had these weird feelings like some dark spell had been cast and broken, and I felt the dangerous, beautiful, feminine world of the Goddess and its sinister tones— that stark contrast of the underworld that I'd fallen into.

She knew how spooked I was by my fall and all and in her caring way with the years of experience she had on me, was my friend, helping me to chill in my skin whilst I figured how to sort my hand out. But in my thoughts I was in the petri dish of the cosmic lab, and visions swept through me of rituals performed by daughters of the dark, sacrificing the Templars and Seekers of the Light. Ageless and secret, I had flashes like I'd been tested using sexual enchantment, and kept having mental images and scenes of dark witchery from some century past. Some twisted karmic wormhole unveiled images of a past life and death, a picture bewitched by second sight. Was it possible that energy that flowed through Maya and I played out in another life and time? It was understood that energy never dies, it just moves into another form. Players on this otherworldly stage, a creative surge from the loins of the universe, had a force, a power, a thrust engineered an act that crossed time? These were powerful thoughts and images and I had this feeling that my life had been taken in a dark ritual. It was so very strange it was to walk around with these thoughts and visions mixed in with my dark and stormy cocktail of endorphins, meditation and Larium.

On rocky ground, beneath thunderous skies, I saw myself flashing in a shard of light, through the cracked mirror, energy bursting in the crystal hall, kneeling in a hood between a conducting rod and a lightning ball. Part of a grander scheme than I could comprehend, in that powerful place of meditation amidst the giant crystals, courtyard and ancient well, all sorts of visions would arise and I was thankful to not be alone in that fearless place.

Feeling like all of us guests had known each other simply by the look in our eyes. The weeks there had been constant Déjà vu and it seemed true that there was a connection between creatures who all travelled independently to the same place in time. Connected on the journey there together, we participated in many worlds and dimensions way beyond our comprehension. With my fucked up hand and all, the sticky essence of those bonds could be seen as well as felt. At the end of myself in wit and wisdom, I went to visit a temple with a couple of friends I made in that place of peace and meditation. We left pre-dawn to arrive there for sunrise, to experience the magic hour before busloads of tourists would surely arrive. Walking into each of the stupas, we saw they each housed a larger than life sculpture of a personified Hindu deity that beamed in stony power in the center of their temple domains. The volcanic stone pumice from which they were carved breathed with fire, light and life. The energy and presence of the thought, infused with the wish in the deep dank musk of stone and incense, I could feel and see the presence of these enchanted beings coming from the light of the astral plane. Making our silent dawn offerings, we walked into one of the temple stupas, which strangely was empty of the presence of stone carved beings, but instead the center of the stone slab floor was lashed with burgeoning morning light.

Standing in that light, alone in the stupa, I noticed two protruding stones on the side walls at around my head height. They were markers, protruding keystones that seemed to project a force. And as I lifted my hands and arms up, reaching out like wings in the direction of these magnetic stones, I closed my eyes. In a sudden beam of vision, the light of my mind spun into a vortex, enormous black feathered wings flapped around me, my head becoming flat, eyes round and piercing, an aerodynamic beak appearing. Opening my eyes, the space was yet again empty, other than the light, and closing them again, there it was, that Great bird of prey, revealing itself within me. This was the Temple of Garuda, the sacred bird. And it was powerful visionary medicine.

Old soul and young fool, exhausted, shattered, peaceful and in pain through this saga, I knew I had to get to a hospital and sort my hand properly before I was in serious trouble. I made a few calls and found out that the best sports medicine hospital in the East was in Singapore. So that evening I was carrying my backpack and taking a seat on a small passenger plane, lifting off at sunset, pack on lap, smoking volcanoes peaking above golden orange clouds.

After a month in Java, it was a reality bite to be suddenly back in a modern city with futuristic highways and buildings in contrast to the small ancient towns of the volcanic tropics. But I was happy to be sitting in a cab that wasn't about to break down, riding to one of the best hospitals in the world—tendons and sports injuries their specialty. Ready for my Singapore Sling, I'd come to the future to be worked on, to set my past right. Arriving late in the night, I couldn't be admitted until my insurance paperwork was thoroughly checked. I sat there in the waiting room as the necessary international calls were made, awaiting a happy ending. Oblivious as I was, I never had been too concerned about the insurance racket, but damn, was I thankful that box was ticked. My lucky ticket had travel insurance attached. Boxes checked, they escorted me royally, prepping me for surgery for a dawn awakening. It had been seven days since the fall, and I was being put to sleep again, this time by a team of doctors in green, peering down at alien me, plotting to cut my hand open to relocate my tendon and bone.

Before coming round in a sweet private suite I remember being wheeled on a gurney through long corridors of the hospital and up to a pristine and heavenly roof with marble columned gates, flowers, and an endless blue sky. Dreaming. It all had a whole other surrealistic golden light about it. And the light got brighter, bluer, whiter, golden, and the Keeper at the Gates there leant over me and said, "Don't worry, everyone who comes here learns to heal."

III. Rites of Passage

I'd thought that my journey would be longer, but cut short after a month, I'd been repatriated. Flown back to Britain a few days after the surgery with my hand slung in a cast and a metal rod to set my finger and knuckle in place whilst it healed. I had stopped taking the Larium and headed from London to Edinburgh—the majestic city where I'd been living and studying. Out of balance, emotionally wonky, buzzing, I was reeling my line in after the storm. It had been one hell of a trip and I was scattered and shattered as could be. The familiar landscape of Britain was settling and it was great to be on me way North again to that place of elemental inspiration that I'd been calling home.

It'd been an enlightening couple of years living there, regardless of my falling out with academia and institutionalized education. There seemed too much to garner from the landscape of people, place and time to be tied to being tested on my knowledge. It seemed a bit phony as an artist to go to college to learn art and find approval and success in the world. What was Art anyway? Something innate or learned. You either had it or you didn't, was my feeling. I kept butting heads with the tutors, my interest in direct experience being too free thinking to be boxed up by an art institution. Especially by an art institution. Living beyond definition, that seemed interesting to me and I wanted to explore ways of seeing, the nature of perception itself.

Formal education also cut too hard into my extracurricular activities and I didn't like to be taught how to paint, how to write. I felt I'd already done my time, learning elements of critical thinking at secondary school—and I couldn't wait to get out of there. I stuck it out 'til I was eighteen just because I felt I had to. But I was done, had enough, and was frankly traumatized by the damn constant tests and papers done by cramming memory. All those years of reading writing and arithmetic were all done by hand, my right hand. Every crayon, pencil, biro, fountain pen and brushstroke mark had been made with the same hand. I hadn't much used computers or really learned to type—it was all scratch and scrawl. Now every mark was a twinge of memory that had been cut in a new line through the palm of my right hand.

Leaving home and London a few years earlier, I had earned my stolen freedom. Taking a year of solo travel, to wing it across North and Central America for what we called a gap year. It was a dream come true I'd plotted since I was thirteen, warning my folks all those years in advance that I would be leaving when I was eighteen, to travel across America for a year, and live the dream. I had the passport, had saved money through all my part time jobs and took off when the time came. Getting into all kinds of adventures for weeks, months and into a year of living solo on the road at eighteen. Most of my friends in London and Edinburgh had also taken some slingshot at freedom, so I wasn't alone in that brave hearted spirit, eighteen being the ripe proper age in blighty to go out and explore the world, see with your own eyes what it was all about.

Coming back was way harder though, like a false break and change of track even though it had been known, been the plan, all along. Stepping back on the conveyor belt from freedom to educational institution was a really tough step to take, a hard pill to swallow. But I'd been awarded a top place on a popular course in the much lauded Edinburgh—and the free education that it was at the time, I thought I'd go live up there for a while and see if I could hack it further with education.

My mates all having travelled different continents during our years of stolen freedom, dinner party conversations through the bone cold winters ignited great ideas and lots of creative passion. The spectral colors of night and unbelievable inspired journeys told sitting around bedroom fireplaces and kitchen hearths of our student flats kept us all warm, entertained and thoroughly illuminated. Many of my mates were interested in deeper knowledge, studying quantum physics, anthropology, comparative religion, literature and the arts. What a great bunch of peers I got to know and call my friends, passing bottomless cups of tea, red wine and hash spliffs.

1993 to '96 were noted by a great broad streak of coincidence, synchronicity that was very apparent to many. We noticed it, talked about it, how pronounced it was. Uncanny coincidence. Intrigued by the gelling web of creative consciousness, our etheric tentacles found wave lengths we never knew existed. Lots of music was made, ten piece jam bands ripped it up 'til the sirens wailed. Deep in music, color, story, some went further—way further, into personal private study of esoterica, tuning into the Gnosis, drinking in The Rose and Cross, amidst psychic and psychedelic exploration. This was a real higher education, as we looked for the Master in the Great Halls, Secret Chapels and Hidden Temples.

Making frequent blustery walks to classes across the meadows, up and down the hills, through the passageways and over bridges, we felt the old town captured the presence of the centuries passed. Hidden mysteries and histories were buried there in that stone city, seeping from the pores of buildings at every turn.

Following the ley lines, the geomagnetic fields and ways, it was told the Templar knights had brought the knowledge and the secret flame of life to Scotland a long time ago. The Ancient ways of Druidic lore could be seen and felt in the prickly gorse, wild grasses and rich red volcanic earth. In the shroud of mist and wind, rugged and wild, a seat of power created there by King Arthur stood on the edge of that hilly city by the sea. Arthur's

Seat. A leonine mountain that hummed through Edinburgh with its inner roar. This was the sun lion's domain.

Shadows lurking in cold damp alleys became seasonally dispelled, the summertime a payoff with its bright white northern light a true gold. A gift to return and climb into that voluptuous red green land, for two years I'd been living there and I climbed Arthurs' Seat at least twice a week regardless of weather, feeling its rhythms and hum, taking drums and didgeridoos out into its rolling hills and crags to party all night with my flat mates and friends in the presence of the nature spirits and moonlight. Embraced by the long grasses and cliff hangs, the rolling drums bounced off rocks and into the winds, sound coming to life in unexpected ways.

Some serious heads out there. Fools like me, psychic adepts, worldly, intelligent, wise and youthful there was a special sauce and secret fire within the bond of our generation. A group of souls shot like many arrows in a great battle at the end of time, the sharpness, direction and piercing qualities of light and mind carried these arrows into other dimensions. The arrow—being perpetual motion—remained still, for else the world would be destroyed. The obsidian tool was born in volcanic waters, vision reflecting the sight of histories past and future in its fiery tip. Crystallizing in youth, this was a time filled with revelation and personal revolutions. Vision was simply a gift and a way to heal a rift that had formed in time. Taking the high road, we glimmered the possibility of some infinite light of consciousness. An uphill climb all the way, we were building stamina for the unpaved roads ahead. With values shifting at the end of the millennia, generation X or—whatever we were being called, were taking stock of a lifetime ahead—looking for a great leap forward to repair what had been spoiled, create a future worth building. The presence of the past a constant inspiration, so much had been written and ignored, buried, and found again. There was a resurgence in esoteric arts, pre-Internet, and there was a big push in mass market publishing with an onslaught of books about spiritual awareness, perhaps just another wave in 10,000 that had come before. Except this time was different.

Fueling the growing hunger in society to find deeper meaning, tribal elders all over the world were wanting the once fiercely guarded secrets of the ancient truths to be known. Medicine people, shaman and false prophets in all kinds of guises crawled out of the grain to share their teachings for humanity and the Earth. Riding the spirit horse of the time, the 7th generation, the Rainbow Warriors, Generation X all knew the flavor of the day, what time it was.

A crucial mix on the brew, we believed in unity, that there was one source of all creation; that all major religions had the same spiritual source; and that all humans were created equal. Diversity of race and culture was seen with appreciation and acceptance, us all recognizing the true peacemakers' role in our diverse world. Focusing on inner study, finding the well of the heart eliminated racial and religious segregation. Color and belief in God—that ineffable higher force that our ancient green friend had taught us—was an intelligent way of nature, showing us how many paths lead to the same end.

Branches of the One tree, if you could see through the bark, the wood and into the grain, you'd know what all people had in common. This is how we were going to find our way home. By climbing this tree. All this we knew and despite our human enforced divisions of politically proliferated racial segregation, it was time for the tribes to gather together and find the way to create peace for the future. Time coded with these thoughts, pushing at the edge of what had come before us, we reached up on tiptoes from the giants' shoulders, trying to touch the next world. We'd come through it many times before, one world to the next.

A new aeon ahead, ever mindful of our impending future, the Earth was still to be 'shaken with both hands', as the Hopi had said. Our 20th century troubles and struggles had come a long way, but life was still being rolled and gambled on loaded dice. Our genome sliced, we were on a cusp of a new millennia and it had all been written, tens of thousands of years ago.

An Axis Mundi, Edinburgh was a global gathering place and in late summer the festival brought out the colors of the world like nowhere else. The windy Athens of the North drew the tribes from all four corners, a massive international creative crowd ripe with good times and great instant friends. My base for the next month, I had to see if I was to stay there and be at college, or split and head back out to the Southwest US desert—a place I'd touched upon a couple of years earlier for some much needed respite, hot springs and healing time. I had to relearn my touch and to use my right fully hand again and I simply needed moons of me time to find my right sense of balance.

Before leaving for Java I'd been painting a lot, seeing if I could conjure a sense of out of body experience in my art. I had my own distinct style and point of exploration in painting, drawing and printmaking, and for some reason that pissed off a few of my tutors and I was nonplussed. It was either me or my work that just didn't appeal to some of them, probably because I was too abrasive, independent, just someone who thought he knew better. I'd look around the room and see twenty different paintings that all looked the same and a teacher that had been educated in the same place. I so vehemently didn't want to be molded. I needed the time to seek and to find my own way. When they'd be looking over my shoulder making suggestions my fire arose and I'd shoot them some arrows from my eyes, self-protective against influence beyond my willing. It felt valid, not just crazy, but I was at a traditional figurative painting and drawing school, more personally inspired by the poetic, surreal, the mystic, discovering new worlds and more into burning than building bridges.

Bull headed, thankfully the printmaking studio down in Leith next to the botanical gardens gave me sanctuary. Letting me give form to some celestial vision of my fiery worlds, and other psychedelic and romantic notions I'd been consumed by. I liked the tutors there. They were artists' artists, not just teachers perpetuating a lame system and infrastructure. And they gave me the elbow room to pursue my thinking. I had plenty of inspiration to keep me occupied and it was best to give me an outlet, rather than telling me to bottle it and do what everyone else was doing. What the hell was the point and purpose of art otherwise? To paint chocolate box images, or be taught how to be audacious?

Ploughing the fields of my heart and mind, I made etchings of misty landscapes incorporating studies at the botanical gardens with abstract forms and cosmic symbolism in my own way. I always used technique as experiment, method and madness conspiring to that wish of greatness, giving form to something timeless and visionary which spoke back. My painting explored lucid surreal visions in still life, landscape and figure, but the light was lighter than life—a trompe l'oeil investigation of fields and color—and I was loving it. But in the year's assessment they had marked me and found me wanting saying I hadn't fulfilled the coursework criteria.

Unjust as I felt that was, it was quite ironic to go to my final fight with a bandaged hand. I planned to meet with the Dean and see what was up with their criteria. I didn't want 'to play the game' any longer and going back to art college in the aftermath of my month long mefloquine madness didn't seem like my best option either. Seeking less restriction, a way to expand my new found psychological pathways, I was pretty sure that college wasn't my way.

Stepping into a magic circle and being given a key to hidden doors, I discovered that fortress of a city was built on seven volcanic hills forged and carved through four ice ages. A geological phenomenon, evolution had made leaps here from the industrial age to the age of enlightenment, since before the plague and its dark and dim ways, the healing arts and sciences had their epiphanies in Edinburgh's Great Halls. Breaking free from those imposing walls I spent much of my free time exploring those hills. Many evenings I'd walk to the top of the hill opposite my flat, whatever the weather, hanging with friends, flat mates or on my own. Calton Hill was always a rugged joy, tempered by the shifting winds.

Called the Athens of the North for good reason, there was a three sided acropolis on the hill top, and a tubular tower with a four way shipping cross. These surrealistic monuments were floodlit for hours of the evening and had amazing views of the ocean, Arthur's Seat, the Castle perched on the volcanic rock and the city all around. Gothic spires pierced clouds and Neo Georgian grandeur bridged it all together royally.

Plenty of times up there on Calton Hill I felt how time travel might be possible, feeling suspended in disbelief at landscape, weather and the sense of history in which my tea bag was steeping. There were many stories dating back centuries about that Hill. It was said there was a gateway to the spirit world, a hidden door to a dimension inhabited by the nature spirits presided over by Pan. The otherworld was mostly unseen by human eyes, but a few had passed through its veils, scribing inspiration and bringing back the knowledge for future generations. Truth be told there were magic hills all over Britain, places where spirits had initiated man in ancient rites of passage. Some of them had been known about for centuries. It was the geomagnetic paths in the earth that linked them and us together. Out of the lodges and secret chapels, rites and rituals were performed, opening wide these hidden doors on hilltops, in cliff sides and glens. These were the secret places and only those with the inner invitation could find their way through.

On Beltane, April 30th of that year, the veils were thinner than perhaps for centuries they'd been. The purifying fires of pagan lore were reenacted, created anew, being performed for a new time as a seasonal ritual on that hill. The ancient Scottish rite set to usher the golden summer dawn, the whole town of Edinburgh welcome, ten thousand strong surged the hilltop in the ceremony procession that night. Hundreds of people painted and garbed as an elemental force—the May Queen, Triple Goddess, White Goddess of the Earth Sky and Underworld guided nature—the Green Man—through his rebirth. A sacrificial initiation, he was to be reborn as a new season, tailed by the Goddesses battalion of white painted garlanded maidens. Flanked by the guarding army of drummers, all hooded with blue painted faces and dressed in black, the procession snaked its way from the steps of the acropolis, weaving its way to the four cardinal points of the hill. Air, Water, Fire and Earth. In each direction the Green Man met his spirit elements, them all coming to life in full painted dance and costumed spirit.

The night set alight with the wish, the dream and the intention of renewal, the public, Calton Hill and City of Edinburgh were all shaken to awaken in this intense performance. Minds and bodies. Flags, spires, flame lit torches, drummers and throngs of people thick with shadows, it was hard not to feel transported. Déjà vu carried me back to medieval times or even earlier. And then the fire spirits of the North came out, hundreds of fire bearing red painted loin clothed writhing beings, dancing devilishly playful humans lusting on the temptation of their role. To breathe new life into time and ignite the season with its fertile spark, the Goddess' maidens sowed the seeds.

Burning through the night, the fires decimated the winter chill in the newly budding season. Reaching for the climax, the Green Man—the elemental—king was stripped bare, all dead matter burned away in white fire as the chrysalis of winter dissolved its icy particles for new signs of life.

The ceremony conducted, ninety-five percent of the crowd sloped away leaving still hundreds of us on that hilltop—hundreds of half-naked pagans playing with fire, running wide eyed and wild. A powerful passion played in the loins of the hill that night and between the blue faced drummers and red naked devils, there were airy creatures with costumed wings, tooting flutes, tingling chimes and penny whistles. Pan was there with his pipes too, flitting around that hill, feet barely touching the ground. Keeping the air alight with sound through the dark night, the soul sacrifice and ceremony of change was about letting go, love and renewal. From moment to moment, I could sense the shift in the night and the season, the elements transforming as the dawn approached. Dark night of the soul, one had to be ever watchful, ever awake in the home of the Horned God. The wilderness of soul set free, Spirit was out in full force that Edinburgh night of the ancient Beltane rite.

Shift by subtle shift, the darkness was breaking one hue of blue at a time. The light overcoming darkness, the edges of color were strung out and frayed at the edge of our spectral visions. I could see the colored hum of light, energy fields shimmering color around my friends, plants, animals and other life forms. In the magenta and green at the cusp of dawn, with the Sun rising up from Arthurs Seat in roaring heat, there in that pre-emergent morning I could see the patterns of light that informed the physical world.

Into the golden dawn and still wakeful, walking home across town, the fire was in my blood and the heat of the sun warmed my skin from the outside in. A rare thing in Scotland, we'd fired up the elements with our ceremony and they'd responded. In fact it was so hot that morning that everything shimmered with heat haze, the heat of the night making a difference in the green world. Man, naked and raw, communicated and let go to be guided by the Goddess, the creator, from his most primal self to his highest calling.

I could see Calton Hill from my bedroom window, it was a smacker of a view. Right there framed by my bay windows on the other side of Waverly Station, my flat looked right onto it. I had a real connection with that place, my front garden—Arthurs Seat being my back yard.

And what with those epic otherworldly nights I'd experienced up there, I really loved that place for all its wide eyed mystery.

In every sense it was pure magic. I'd be sitting in my room watching the light of day constantly change around the crazy architectural monuments, and I'd always notice when the lights would turn on and off. They didn't seem like they were on a timer, always happening at a different hour but it did start to get strange though, as I'd find myself look out the window and they would go on or off right at that moment. And then I started testing it by saying 'on' / 'off' in my mind or aloud in my quiet room and looking at it with intent, the light on the tower and shipping cross strangely responded to my will, "On / off, on / off" I started to play with it like a little kid with a new trick. Far out it was, then I started to take it a little personally.

Falling down that mystic rabbit hole, I consumed esoteric texts and art books practically by osmosis, spending deep Scottish winters mixing and matching light moons of Magritte and other Magi—Blake, Baha-ullah, Lao Tsu, the Tao Te Ching, the I Ching, the Tarot and the Rune stones. It was quite a diet of archetypes, symbolism, studying the ancient practices of divination. It fascinated me, this personal psychoanalysis or hippie poker like we called it. These obscure arts held a great deal of insight and with my powerful spark I was in uncharted personal territory, a novice initiate learning to navigate a lesser known way.

The hardest thing to get my head around was how to understand, let alone relate, the insights I was having. So deeply intimate, all the elements were universal but that far out universe was not a common exploration. It was hard not to feel a bit alienated in my rare experience, but that was nothing new, always having taken my own path far away from the crowd. Thankfully here though were peers on something of kindred journeys, and whilst it was all so hard to put into words, a few close friends remained by my side. So I continued to go deeper down that rabbit hole whilst most of our fellow students were just happy to get drunk and fuck around. But for some reason, I kept listening to that calling that rang in my ears, unable to ignore it and prepared to make that sacrifice to find meaning and purpose in my life. To understand the subtler truths and secret nature of reality that kept so well hidden out of sight and view. It wasn't just about splashing around in backwaters, I wanted to be in the true river of life lifted by the flow, not just jump into the polluted mainstream to be pulled along and down by undertow.

Being at Art college was really a whole other kettle of fish—practically a distraction from my bizarre unfolding way. I was always going to paint, sculpt, draw—make art. Needing to work with my hands in that way— as medicine and communion, I had to do it to be at peace with the world. Playing with lightning, looking for the keys to knowledge, I remember hearing what Ben Franklin had said—that 'Genius without education was like silver in the mine.' I just didn't enjoy feeling skinned alive by the educational institution. Banging my head against a wall since I was a kid with that, working hard to get out my inspiration, I was always being knocked down for doing it my own way rather than by prescription. Stubborn, impetuous, bull headed, it seemed to me the popular pill kept minds dull and the world boring, controlling the many for the benefit of the few.

Taught to believe in meritocracy at a young age, we were told if we worked hard enough at what we loved we could do or be anything we wanted. I just never figured that I'd be at Art College, ending up there by default, having quit the University. Studying History of Art and Anthropology, alongside all the studio arts in a joint honors program, it was considered prestigious. All that left and right brain conjoined Da Vinci stuff—and out of two thousand applicants, I'd got one of the twenty places. But in practical terms it meant double the workload and that was a monkey on my back that I was all too ready to shake off.

I knew what I didn't want more than what I did, so I chipped away at the structures until nothing was left to contain me and all I had to do was pick up my bag and move on. I wanted to mine my silver streaks of illumination, find those keys, and being back in Edinburgh during the festival I knew without shadow that my education had been the city and my friends. Keen to avoid the wet cold that would sink into me through another dark Edinburgh winter, I resolved that I'd pack up my stuff and leave Edinburgh at the end of August, giving up my room with the prize view there to a friend, and head toward a necessary healing episode in my surreal life, heading west to brave the new world.

IV. Star Waters~Earth Ships

The Land of Enchantment. The desert always had its healing draw. A barren place filled with hidden life and shimmering haze where illusions were all burned away. "Go west" the voice had whispered and I had listened. Flying to Albuquerque, the 'querques as it was affectionately known, Road Runner and Wil' E Coyote had Acme dynamited the place into my consciousness. 'I'm not a Coyote, I'm you', read the sign. I figured any place with that many U's—considering their striking from the American language in color, honor, labor and humor, seemed to deserve a little attention.

Drawn in further, I was going out back into the southern boonies of New Mexico, headed for the bizarre and auspiciously named Truth or Consequences that hid in plain sight. Stepping down off the Greyhound bus just past the highway off ramp, the morning was bright and the desert sky vast. Southern New Mexico. Burning into my eyeballs, the golden ochre, sienna hues and endless vistas seen in so many westerns came to life again as I walked from the outskirts of the town to the travelers hostel on the banks of the Rio Grande. For ten bucks a night I could wake up in a teepee and bathe in mineral hot springs morning and night. What about that wasn't appealing?

I figured I could chill there for a bit and get my bearings in the desert southwest US. Small town America with its unpaved streets, trailers, 1950s siding and similar pre-fab housing. I was out of my element, a nowhere man, and I was happy to be there. I hadn't cut my hair in months nor shaved in a while either. I carried my didgeridoo I had picked up in Edinburgh from an Aboriginal traveler with a market stall, and I had a small pack with a sleeping bag wrapped in a ground sheet. My wardrobe was limited simply to the clothes on my back, though a couple of pairs of socks, boxers and a t shirt or two, didn't add any real weight to the baggage I carried. I really didn't mind wearing the same jeans day in and out, washing them every week. They just got better all the time. My hiking boots also held up pretty well, built to last better in that day. I was a free bird, traveling solo being both easy and necessary for my inner growth.

Back then—the mid 90s, there were plenty of people from all over the world traveling across the US. An archetypal vision propagated by the likes of Jack Kerouac and Hunter S Thompson, I reckoned they would have appreciated my journey. I was running to life, away from so called society. In our insane world it was true that only the sane are insane. On a healing trip in the desert of the real, I was thankful to be a few steps beyond the illusions and mental confines of contemporary society. The decade may have been different but the mind set was the same, and I aimed my sights beyond the endless strip malls of Arby's, Denny's, Dairy Queens, Burger Kings and McDonalds which lined every highway and through fare. The homogenizing culture had us incorporated up to our necks yet still hadn't yet entirely consumed us, there being a few moments of grace before the propaganda that would brand the end of time, would steal most civilized minds. There was still the land and the sky beyond—and enclaves, bastions and outposts of independence within.

Welcome to T or C, as they called it. A free radical mindset was able to be sought, the lost still around to be found. Previously named Hot Springs (Ojo Caliente), I quickly discovered that (as to be expected in America) the town took its name after a 1950^s game show, which offered $50,000 to any place willing to wear it. The whole town had gathered, voted and with pride won the prize to wear the tag. The writing was on the wall. Way back when, before it was Apache territory, it was home to prehistoric Indians and woolly mammoth. More recent western history witnessed it as a place where warring tribes would call Peace, and lay down their weapons for a while to heal their wounds in the magically charged mineral waters. All this amidst the violent and bloody legacy of frontier history. It wore the name well. But what you saw on the surface were churches with drive through sign-posts, yards filled with beaters—old Chevys and Cadillacs on bricks sans wheels or doors; mangy desert dogs barking behind chicken wire fences and other archetypal parodies of small town American life.

Yet at the bend in the river on the edge of town was a remarkable place. A traveler's oasis. Behind the gravel forecourt surrounded by alligator cottonwood trees stood a world apart. Beyond the pre-fab ranch houses and trailers used for accommodations, there were decks, a dock and small coves tucked away in the trees that lined the river. Some of the guests stayed for a night or two passing through on their way east or west, while others became more permanent, staying for weeks or months at a time. Some worked a few hours a day in trade for their bed, in return they became the family like community that maintained both the spirit and mortar of the place. For travelers who had been on the road for many months, sometimes years, this small town on the edge of nowhere became a destination. Usually their story involved a strange magnetic pull or a desire to return. I had passed through a couple of years earlier and for some good reasons, I couldn't stop thinking about it. Perhaps this seemingly obscure rest stop held keys to hidden knowledge. Maybe it was all in the waters, the opportunity to suckle at the bosom of imagination in the desert of the real.

Truth was, and I was a little lost. I needed to sit still long enough in that big wide open to know myself again. If I walked around in circles in the same spot for awhile, I might even find out where I was at. Haunted by the earlier months of mayhem in my life, I knew that this was a new beginning, a place to get my bearings and find guidance for the life that awaited ahead. Putting my bag down and walking over to the river and covered deck that housed the mineral baths, I just sat and watched the river and the sky, waiting for the mineral baths to be filled, to soak the twisted knots of my body and mind away. Emptied and filled twice daily, when I climbed into the baths in the desert dusk I felt so much tension begin to be lifted. Deep disharmonies downright disintegrated, the doors to all my locked away resentments began to be opened, wounded sensitivities embraced by the bubbling warm waters. It was amazing how utterly closed off I was. I had knots tighter than tight, roping and tethering me to my interpretation of reality.

Relearning to use my right hand, and trying to understand the things that had been happening, my heart cried out in love, feeling like the whole affair in Java was part of some magical ritual and I was a mystic probate, making a sacrifice as part of an even larger story. Was Maya an emanation of the Goddess I had met on that black sand beach? I felt like we'd been seduced by a potent force much greater than ourselves, guided together to experience an explosive force, an awakening force ten times greater than any force of Love, I knew. Three-hundred kilovolts, pure lightning. But what did I know? How many excuses could I find to understand my fumbles and blunders?

In that moment of conception, the warp speed roller coaster through the wormhole had sent me to the center, to glimpse the pulsing origin and source of life. Pushed over the edge of myself and falling back around to the beginning, I had this deep interminable emptiness welling inside, knowing that I'd conceived a child in that moment with Maya. Oh Java! Before leaving Britain again, I'd received a heartfelt letter from her, confirming our intuition and saying that she decided to terminate the pregnancy. Hard as that decision was she wrote she felt it was for the best. I admit I felt relieved first and empty second, being twenty-one and not nearly ready nor wanting to be a father yet. But the emptiness haunted, a present but absent spirit of life hung over me.

There too—in that place I kept remembering her. Those other piercing eyes that seemed to be watching and protecting me with love. Who was she? This beautiful enigma who existed deep in my memory. I knew her and I didn't. Was she someone with whom I had made a pact to meet again? Where did these thoughts, feelings, visions and memories come from? Was it beyond life? Before this after life? Who knew how far back it dated—stored in the archives of time, or when it might make sense again. This essential feeling that I couldn't escape was true love and I was looking for it. Was she a guide or soul mate? A twin flame, someone who maybe I knew from the space womb, from the petri dish of Time? So connected to this parallel force, I was in limbo, existing purely in my heart and mind between worlds, beyond questioning what was real.

As the night encroached and the stars appeared, my mind drifted and I began to feel lighter. The minerals working their magic, Sodium, Calcium, Potassium Magnesium, Chloride, Bicarbonate, Silicate, Silicon— minor traces of Lithium, Barium and Uranium, amongst others in the New Mexican earth. Alchemical waters.

Restoring my strength and balance, sleeping under canvas and the seventeen poles that held up the teepee universe, my heart and mind were easing up, feeling at one with my surroundings with just the thinnest of veils separating my inner and outer worlds.

That night it happened, I took a desert flight. Drifting into dream under the canvas teepee cone, I lifted upwards, seeing through birds eyes as I soared over the town, exploring the area with my Garuda's eye view. This was new, but would become habit. Everyone has flying dreams at one point or another, but since I left Java, I found I would go fly whenever I slept in a new place just to get familiar with the ley of the land. I knew it was more than a dream, as even from a great height with my eagle eyes I'd see all the topography, town layout, street lights, shop signs, trash in gutters, running cats and parked cars, and I'd recognize them when I walked around over the next few days, noticing the strangest of details as memories in place.

The desert light and expanse was quite the magical terrain to explore, revealing the light of creation—as a bird, four legged, two legged, or crawling creature. Swooping through sandstone and granite canyons, and over the mountains there to White Sands, at dawn I glided over the crystalline gypsum topography—close to the ground—under radar. Invisible in the land of my vision, everything appeared magenta, ultra violet, as I swept and slithered over the microcosmic magenta world of the endless white in the dawn light.

As day broke, I awoke to the birdsong, the sound of the river and the flowing waters, the tubs on a timer being filled with the hot spring waters. Mists and minerals evaporating into the morning light and air, I could see her eyes—my timeless guide, the unknown beauty in my heart and mind. I had given myself to her and I kept hearing a voice telling me have no fear. In glimpses of wonder, I had seen this journey since I was a nipper. Perhaps I always knew I would meet my destiny and that she would know my true name. I'd asked for her in my dreams. At the volcanoes edge and the temple of the four winds. On the red road through the valley. I whispered to her at dawn and dusk. Called out to her silently by the river. At midnight in the caves, through the witching hour in the graveyard and at dawn in the secret garden. Even in the cities I'd seen her eyes in my dreams and in the magazines. The planetary Goddess had swallowed me up, popping my otherworldly cherry. One woman, she had many different faces.

Beyond the concrete reality and high rising smog of most American life, the simple pleasure of desert sunsets, glowing mountains, healing waters and life on the river was enough—at least for a little while. That was the thought creeping into me. I had been there for a few days and could feel the pace in my gait easing up, my innate bustle and hustle subsiding. It was hard to refute the lulling pleasure and tingling sensation that seeped into my bones. Hot springs. Flowing waters. All those minerals with reactive properties had a transformational effect, encouraging deep introspection, relaxation and you better believe it, well-being. People came to this place precisely for that reason, and it deserved its reputation as a healing place.

The first time—years earlier—I sat in those waters filled with hundreds of trace minerals breaking upwards from the ground below, a handful of people had appeared covered in dry caked mud, talking about just having been in a sweat lodge. I was really curious about what on earth they were talking about. Native ceremonies? Indian prayer lodges? Nothing in my experience at the time could help me understand that world. They talked of Eagle medicine and an earth ship—a project being worked on down river on a mesa at the site of a prehistoric native settlement. Of course I was intrigued to learn much more about this new world. That's what had drawn me back there years later.

So with the peaceful waters I remained, one night turned into a week, at which point I decided that I should work a few hours or whatever was needed in trade for a place to sleep. Happy to get the opportunity to work on the mesa project, every morning after a sunrise soak on the deck over the river, a few of us would pile into a truck and roll along the dusty desert dirt road over the bridge, off road bumping, rocking and scratching on the single track five miles down. Some days we'd catch the current, taking the small boat down the Rio Grande, docking nearby in a cottonwood grove to walk the final stretch to the site. About two thirds of the way was a lightning struck tree, a burnt grizzled stump that always attracted vultures to perch. Our cartoon signpost of the arid territory it was obvious how vital water was in the desert—the green river a precious life force.

Desert skies forever vast, the reflective shining blue burnished the oceans of golden desert sands. My first time on the mesa, there were hundreds of recycled old bald tires of different shapes and sizes that had been stacked at the site. They'd begun to be laid out in a shallow excavated pit, but I still couldn't picture the shape of things to come. Ramming them with earth and pounding them with sledge hammers, I quickly realized what a damn back breaking labor project I'd signed up for, still clueless as to the end we were beginning, nevertheless along for the ride. Pounding dirt in the desert out there in New Mexico under the blazing sun I had an epiphany. I understood what Aldous meant when he wrote about the savage reservation and the Brave New World in which I was raised, where I read of the Soma which I was fed, but hadn't digested it all. My world view was shifting and I was slowly being reborn in the desert.

We rammed earth in the midday sun. Building blocks, making structurally reinforced walls out of earth, a pod, a dome was being created, buried in the ground. Built to even withstand earthquakes. Tires were used for strength and their availability was embraced as part of an effort to recycle waste materials. For Ezy—a bear of man who owned the oasis, this was his project, his baby, intent on building an underground ceremonial chamber he likened to a Kiva—a space used by native shamans to initiate youth on their path into the mystic world. I was building a dream sanctuary—a place I would return to on my journeys between worlds, working hard on my own inner architecture.

One of those enchanting days, I met Two Bulls, a native elder with braids in his hair, leathered lips and saddlebags beneath his eyes. His way favored what he called coyote medicine—basically natural 'remedies'— or 'tools' as he called them—plants with psychoactive properties. He invited a few of us over to his camp on Mezcal Drive by Elephant Butte Lake. In his trailer we ate, drank, heard stories and later partook in a potent concoction of 'good medicine tea'—as Two Bulls called it—a brew of marijuana, opium, peyote and mushrooms whilst sitting round the fire outside. Besides Two Bulls and Ezy Blackbear, Luke Blue Feather came around and Eddie Three Eagles rode in on his iron horse named Harley Davidson. The spitting image of Geronimo, his ferocious steely eyes, physique and aura extended way beyond his body, but his warm smile and generous spirit was utterly disarming. There was Barney Rhodes too—a slight fellow with a wiry way and wispy whiskers, an underestimated force in the shifting nature of things. His story was a wide meandering river—having lived in Colorado, he'd painted the finest and most ornate of interiors and ceilings of starry celestial visions seen most commonly in the Templar and Masonic temples, but employed by the uber rich when money was water and needed to be frozen into the rafters of the third and fourth homes and mountain estates. Having not got paid by absent owners too many times, he had disappeared off to Alaska and made dog sleds for a living until the cold cut into his bones and he had migrated south for the seasons, making his dog sleds in the Truth or Consequences desert surrounded by hot springs.

Cracking jokes and sharing stories of the Apache who had inhabited the area, as it happened the region was once one of Geronimo's haunts. The only peaceful years of a warring life, hanging with his Chiricahau cousins, Geronimo and his band of renegades feasted, danced, and healed in the hot springs, wanting his remains to be placed in the Gila wilderness in his afterlife. But Geronimo's skull was stolen from his imprisoned burial place at Fort Sill, Oklahoma, by pledges for the Yale fraternity and secret society Skull and Bones. Allegedly the tomb raiding mission was led by Prescott Bush in 1918, when they stole and kept the War Chief's skull as an occult prize of power.

The bones of the medicine man and last free brave still remained in the New Haven tomb, the native deal broken for centuries into the afterlife by the secret rulers and their institutions of great influence. The spoiled seed, those few young chiefs and entitled scions would inherit the Earth from their great granddaddies who stole it, learning to exploit and letting nothing stop their way.

Late that night, when the good medicine tea was done and it was time to go I decided to walk back along the river to the teepee at the hostel, instead of catching a ride. Seems like I had a thing for taking hikes alone through the desert at night. Under the stars and influence of the sweet tea, the night became a wolf, the moon its third eye and the mind of the universe opened wide. Heart and mind shot into a whole 'other' sense of realization, the light and night became liquid, pulsing with energy, the stars flickering, coming closer in their indeterminate distance. As I walked past a small orchard of baby trees and I felt so drawn to the life force within. A fire in my belly, the center of my soul felt connected, drawing me ever closer. To feel life, its green aliveness within trees and plants in the sparse and arid southern New Mexico landscape, that was bliss.

Standing beneath a lamppost by a few houses in a tiny riverside neighborhood my connection to the light was so strong that psychoactive night, I could switch it on and off with the same force of energy, feeling the electricity within my center and controlling it with my will—that ability which had first showed itself in Scotland, growing stronger within. It was an intoxicating state beyond my so called normal everyday reality. And there were the dogs locked up behind gates and fences who could feel my presence as I walked alone under the eye of the great wolf, barking vehemently as I passed by. The sound shook and stirred me to my animistic core, standing there in space, desert space, my mind aglow, awake and at home in a realm of shape shifting shaman and far out worlds.

A pipe ceremony had been planned for the earth ship project on the mesa beneath Turtleback Mountain. The pipe had first been given to the native peoples in a dream. It was a way for the migrating tribes to keep in touch with the creator at all times, granting the means to communicate personal and universal prayers. The ceremony for the kiva dome—the earth ship we were creating was to be strictly Eagle medicine—sky relative of the coyote medicine we'd imbibed a few nights earlier. Ezy wanted to have a peace circle to honor the past, the spirits of that land—and to sail his earth ship over the rocky waves smoothly into the future. The gathering was held in the barren brush of the desert mesa, a circle of twelve. The light was so bright it was hard to see skin color, just shades of clay and earth as we sat in solemnity beneath the sky. It was a simple gesture of love and thanks directed to the North, South, East and West. The pipe passed around the circle five times before the mixture of barks and native tobacco was ash. The first two rounds I was instructed to decline taking it as a mark of respect to the circle—to be properly introduced to the ceremony. On the third, fourth, and fifth round, I lifted the pipe to the sky above, spoke my prayer of thanks before drawing the long cedar stem to my lips. I drew in the smoke, blowing it forth along with my prayer before passing it on, peace fluttering without hesitation.

Amazing that the red pipe stone could hold the flame and keep burning on its starting light, one spark of fire held so many wishes, sharing the flame, intention and prayer with a circle of people. When it was done, everyone said, 'Aho! Mitaqui oysin', 'We are all related.' Then we all took seeds—planting corn that was red, white, black and yellow, in the four directions. The squash, sunflower and onion seeds we planted in circles and spirals in the freshly tilled mineral rich earth was so rewarding in its small way, and fed me in ways I didn't expect.

Rolling into new unknowns, one of those days exploring that territory I climbed down a kiva ladder in an uninhabited thousand year old pueblo built into a hillside. Standing beneath the opening to the sky in the earth pit house it started snowing. Snowfall in the high desert was dry and crisp, the cleansing air, whispering wisps of light and grace had a natural and unexpected mystic to it. To great surprise upon climbing up the ladder to the hole in the sky, the sunshine and clear desert horizon abounded, the snow cloud so localized that all around at a distance, was clear, super cerulean blue dazzling through the white flurries. How striking it was to have so much space to reflect upon the shifting light, the elements, and myself.

My inner vision was growing exponentially, embracing the vastness of the new world. In the landscape of my dreaming soul, that night I camped in a rock shelter near the old pueblo. Hidden beneath the surface of the land a revelation was just beginning to awaken from a spell. A seed had been planted perhaps in aeons past, sitting dormant as stone, fossilized dinosaur DNA waiting for the conception of a fertile mind. Time coded under the measure of an atomic clock that night I fell deeply into dream.

Lucid, I became completely conscious and 'awake' within the dream, having an out of body experience. Walking through tunnels of blanketing darkness, all pervading light rippled in waves through my synapses. Magnetizing my atoms into stardust memories, I stood on the dark turning planetary sphere, alone, walking towards the golden disc, a burning white celestial body of light. Forward, into, straight along the ever turning way, the sphere moved like a treadmill beneath my feet as particles of diamond dust shattered my mind. Eclipsed, a corona emanated around the sun, and I in self-dissolution and oneness with the cosmos, stepped through the eclipse.

Seven eclipses of the Sun and four eclipses of the Moon, the naturally occurring DMT in my brain had broken through floodgates and the city of my past—the concrete structures of self cracked away, as I stood on the edge of the known universe looking into a ball of white fire. I could see clearly the oneness and nothingness, integration and dissolution, our circle of never ending darkness and light. Beyond the shimmering heat of this white-hot horizon the lingering ether was infused with teachings of lost civilizations and reality buried so deeply within illusion as to become fiction.

Nothing is ever as it seems and the truth was indeed stranger. No stranger danger, still there was no thing nor one to fear. Opening my eyes as night turned to day, I found myself back in my body again. I felt different. Pinching my arms, legs, body and mind, I felt like something else had entered. There was an acute awareness present, a little more conscious that I was driving a vehicle that I called my body. I had a thought in my head that wasn't altogether mine, I don't know where I'd heard it, but it seemed old time familiar, coming up from somewhere deep in these atomic stardust memories and taking on new meaning.

The light of the Moon be the light of the Sun, and the light of the Sun be sevenfold, as the light of the seven days.

V. Clowning Around

Three-hundred kilovolts, lightning had followed me and I started to take it personally. Electrifying energy ran through me, crazy weather patterns moved continents in my wake and welcome. Departing London in a lightning storm, landed me in Java. London—New York—Albuquerque, into the wilds of New Mexico and Colorado, the lightning bookmarked my way.

Slowly surely recovering my hand from the accident, I was learning to use it again, finding subtle motion and a new feeling in touch and movement. I started carving semi-precious stones, that tactile feeling, and connection with stone, the way it captures heat, coolness, light and energy. Studying light in the sky and in the earth, the light of the endless day and night, its seven days and rays, its octave filled night of crystal light, I could hear the chimes sing out through the stars. A landscape filled with raw gems, I studied these lesser learned lessons, schooled by nature in the hidden ways of watching, observing, seeing.

Daddy O Sky my Master, Mama Earth my Mistress, and I a son of a gun, shot into this desert ocean.

Nothing in New Mexico was quite what it seemed. You just don't get it on the surface. The Land of Enchantment truly came to life when you closed your eyes. It was the timeless, mythic and spiritual place that exists within your dreams and subtler perceptions. You can smell the pine, the sage, the cedar, the juniper, the amber pitch, the endless shades of earth clays—but the rustic beauty, expansive space and mystic light was so thick you had to cut a slice.

The electrical energy in the desert was high, humming, and so was I. I could feel the heat build through the afternoon, getting ready to crack, a mind so full of tension it had to split open—Athena piercing her way out of Zeus' head. Looking up into the pregnant looming clouds of the violet sky, bolts of light forked in the dusky twilight—not grounding—just arcing this way and that, I seemed to be able to tune into it. A precognitive spark, I could feel where it would burst next. Plugged into a high voltage source, sensing and feeling the force just moments before each thrust of energy illuminated the sky. Conductor in a cosmic symphony, pointing with my eyes into the 360 dome of infinite space, I played in the celestial song, the sizzling sensation of the electrical reaction tuned into with my psychic tendrils. Cosmic crescendos, cascading light, shards of sound, and chimes of glass, dreams of future selves, echoed in eternity as they waited to be born, one day striking the ground.

In one brief moment of reflection I closed my eyes, when suddenly my mind and body turned vermillion in a flood of burning red orange beneath my eyelids. Spilling inward like a gallon of paint poured onto my inner canvas, the force of light, heat, and energy was so powerful, rocket fire thrusting me backward off the log on which I was perching. I could taste the electricity, that metallic taste in my teeth and lips. Just a few feet away the ground smoldered.

Even camels remembered the gatherings at the oasis. Having travelled from T or C into the high desert of Northern New Mexico, late one lucid night after being out at a bar—La Vida—under the shadow of Taos Mountain, I ran into two brothers I had met in the south. Darien and Clay were two young dreadlocked hippy hobos who had a thing for taking mushrooms and getting wild beyond themselves. They got loose, unrestrained, and were happy to always take reality further with psychedelic substances. There were madmen on the edge of town. The doors blown off, they had walked through. With their spiraling consciousness, they embodicd spirits that haunted and taunted not only in dreams. They'd cross lines, the invisible ones we draw around ourselves, their Kokopelli like play often unleashed on unsuspecting friends or unwitting bystanders. Blame it on the earth, it was near impossible to not feel swallowed up by the atmosphere of the high desert. No stranger danger. From the earth into the next world, tearing through the fabric in the mesh of reality, I encountered those twisted roots as I walked to my car, them both perched bird like on a limb of a cottonwood tree beside the road. I was surprised by their shadowy forms and became the sudden target and audience of their moon light taunt. Testing, testing, the way of the clowns… and they did. Dancing around me with a push and pull.

"You're not from here… what are you doing here? Where's your home?… you're from Mars… go home!… what makes you think you're human?… humans wouldn't do that, humans couldn't do that!… go home Mars!… You're from Mars. Go back home…"

With their long dreaded hair sticking out this way and that and barefooted staccato, electric jolting prance of a dance, trousers rolled up, faces cast in shadow, there was something distinctly menacing about their way, their approach and demeanor. I had in fact enjoyed some sober conversations with them, but this was an 'other' story, a kind of magic and energy at work. All I could do was be still and listen, watching my back, trying to be fearless in the threatening face of their audacious fire, circling and lunging towards me with their crazy, repetitive taunts.

Mars! Who knows? Not everyone on this planet is from this planet and that night was particularly alien. The high desert was both twisted and curved. You could see the frayed edges at the fringe of the old tight weave. It had plenty of warps and even a few holes—but those edges revealed all kinds of secrets. Something about that mountain and the Taos hum, it made things unravel if they weren't tightly threaded. It brought out that inner fire too. It certainly wasn't hum drum, many rhythms and strangely intriguing melodies were being played.

The following morning I met a dude named Des as I was picking up a coffee at a local hangout. A gregarious character with an infectious yet pensive personality, I would never have guessed by his look that he was full blooded Native American. Wearing baggy jeans and a football shirt, he wore a bandana strapped around his head and looked a bit like a Chicano gangster. Standing apart from all association, his pale skin, jet black hair and blue green eyes were jarring. Stocky in build, broad nose, wispy facial hair and round jaw gave him the air of a Mongolian warrior—perhaps only the black braids made any allusion to native roots. But those were just my snap second shots, my insta-take on this dude. I don't know how we got talking, it came pretty naturally, hitting it off quickly, drinking coffee in a yard on the edge of the road going in and out of town. It was one of those funny senses of knowing that arise from old friendships and sometimes amongst kindred spirits, brothers of sorts. Despite our completely different backgrounds, we hit a point of commonality and found a lot of laughter and wacky insight in one another.

Sometimes dudes need buddies more than girlfriends and that kind of camaraderie was priceless and very valuable to me, rolling solo through the big sky land. We both found ourselves there having been tumble dried in similar cycles of heartbreak. On our own healing trip, carrying heavy baggage from our trespasses with the earth and womankind. So there we both were, raw and open, pondering and speculating on what the fuck we were thinking by walking into the heat of our fires only to be left out in the cold. And more importantly how the hell would we put ourselves back together.

Hanging out all hours of the night talking shit, watching the fire and making music in the desert moonlight, more tangibly intangible there was something else about our connection. More than our mutual twisted heart bullshit there was something about energy, about lightning, that I was learning. All those powerful encounters with electrical and spiritual forces I'd been having for a couple of years, I hadn't found much help or any real roadmaps to guide or provide me with any direct answers or insight. But I began to discover a bit of true knowledge in my new pal Des. The more time we spent together, the more he opened up with the stuff that was the glue of his cultural background and I was discovering first hand all sorts about shamanic practices—the root knowledge of his clan. The Clown clan.

Certainly a peculiar kind of energy and magic punctuated my existence. On too many occasions earlier in my life, the girls that I found a mutual attraction with were literally kept at bay by our amazing and illuminating spark. It was like a touch fired up all our shit, and to be plugged into that kind of energy source or have that plugged into you, may have seemed appealing but rarely lasted longer than a night at a time. Pushing the buttons to the point of total awareness, most people didn't want to be seen. That was the difference with Maya, but it was me who had fucked up. To be truly seen as we were and are, not as we tried to model ourselves. It was like an electrical conduit climbed deep inside and wiggled around 'til it found the most tender of spots, giving you a good zap from the inside out.

It wasn't much fun not being able to get closer to those you really felt a connection with. Love was deep, profound and instant, karma pushed buttons, electrifying and enlightening, making you feel more alive, awake and brighter than ever imagined, and with the same intensity it could consume, frazzle you to a crisp leaving you more desolate and alone than you could ever fathom. Sad and lonely was unfortunately part of the warriors' path. For without that, it was hard for true sensitivity, passion and purpose to bloom. Soul still needed fertile ground out of which to grow. This was the kind of nonsense that Des and I would talk about sitting by fires out there in the desert nights, free camping, living rough by hot springs, making music and listening to the stars, feeling like the watchers and the watched. Sleeping out there one night under the starlight I dreamed of the future, and I remembered. I went up in a craft to a space port, and then entered into a clear bubble capsule and floated in the stars gravity free, suspended at night in the cosmic origin, I saw the ever present future and I remembered. I saw the light in her eyes and I felt the all-consuming love of it all, my spirit and soul seeming to swell, holding the world in mutual embrace. Enfolded in the desert mystery under the arc of the vast night, those sparkling eyes of the sky, she who I knew through all time and space was out there, and I knew I would one day find her again.

Des and I traveled together to pueblos and places I would never have found or had access to on my own.

Catching rides along the way, in every place he had cousins and relatives. We were invited to eat at family tables, food I couldn't decipher in places that transported me right out of the Upper 48 and back into simpler times of way less development. The reservations and pueblos we visited played with all my notions of time and space. Indian time and space being quite different, I embraced the warp in the weave of the fabric of time as the place where Spirit entered.

At the source of our lives as earth dwellers, despite the bottles of Coca-Cola, beer and the usual trash of the modern world strewn about the place, life and its ways had remained pretty much the same lifetime after lifetime. Meeting Des' cousins, the clown clan, they painted themselves black and white in horizontal stripes with flashes of red in bandanas and ribbons, embodying the spirits of thunder and lightning. A whole other joke of black, white and read all over, these guys always had news for you.

Their role in the dance ceremonies was basically to mess with people and their attachments to both material and spiritual things, ideas, possessions, attitudes and emotions. They'd force you to check yourself, pay attention, and be aware. All of it would be tested and cajoled, pushed and shoved. In the public dances, they'd run out into the crowd, stealing cameras, hats and bags, and climb to the top of a thirty foot pole, standing there on one leg, fearless and wide eyed, keeping in alignment the precarious balance of nature. Dancing with jagged movements they acted as if the world was backwards and to move forward things had to be shaken up. In the ever present past, the Clowns were also the great fearless warriors and shaman, the sad and lonely clowns at the heart of the battles and healing ceremonies, traveling far into themselves to bring back teachings from 'the other world.' They communicated with their ancestral spirits constantly, acutely aware of the shoulders on which they stood and what they were reaching for.

Testing their mettle by enduring painful, piercing and proving trials, with the absence of warring tribes and because of the proliferation of alcoholism, the sweat lodge and Sundance ceremony were a good way profound spirits kept themselves on track, giving a purpose and focus to life by reaching back into their personal cultural identity. Des was exactly this kind of soul. He had related to me how he had strayed so far from his roots as a teenager, getting deep into booze and trouble, hustling in pool halls, the live wire that he was had the rare ability of telekinesis. Moving pool balls on the table with his mind and drawing things to him in spooky ways was natural. It was his trouble with alcohol and police— not such a great combination—that brought him back to the fold and made him realize how valuable his traditional native ways were; to help him understand and know himself as part of a larger puzzle. His story wasn't far different from many of his kin. When not part of the tribe, it was too easy to disappear in the madding crowd of the lost world. A missing piece, a perfect shape cut out and removed from a big picture.

Northern NM had a deep history and heritage of unlikely Anglo artists that had been drawn to the region.

Perhaps I was just another piece in that wandering artist puzzle, linking the spirit of the past to the present. I certainly fell into the landscape, bathed in her waters and dirt. I loved it and felt immersed in the womb of her inspiration. I knew I was not alone, and having uprooted from my own origins, I was finding a path, the direction of my magnetic fields. The artist's way, way of the warrior, the path of Shambhala, I wasn't the only one looking for Shangri La. Wanderers, seekers, artists, and fools, I wondered if they too had beer bottles thrown at them by drunks driving by in pickups with gun racks when hitchhiking on the side of the road. Or if when swimming in the Rio Grande, did DH Lawrence or Aldous Huxley have rocks rain down around them from unseen hands? Perhaps Georgia O'Keefe encountered the inter-dimensional Sasquatch in the early morning mist down by the Arroyo Hondo Hot Springs?

Some phenomena were understood but remained closely guarded secrets by Des and his cousins. They weren't anxious to put these stories into words, but they could see my mark, the fire and light that burned in me. They saw what I needed more than I could comprehend. So as a visitor from a faraway land who needed a rarely sought form of guidance, I was welcomed—a rare blessing for a stranger to be invited to sacred ceremony at the Pueblo. Not many outsiders had ever participated in these intensely secretive and sacred ceremonies in that ancient place of deep belonging. Not part of the visitor's tour, for many it was completely taboo for me to be there, but equally this clan of crazy clowns made no qualms about inviting me into their community as a brother making a personal rite of passage. I know they related to my stories of Scotland, and said that I was one the fire people of the North, and that I needed to understand and know. Naturally, that just drew me deeper, intrigued to know what I couldn't comprehend. All things in spirit being equal, still I had to hide down in the back seat of the truck as we passed a security inspection by the tribal police at the entrance into the private residence area of the thousand year old pueblo.

On Indian time, I hung out in a two room simple house—a basic primitive dwelling with terracotta tile floors, mud brick walls, power fed by a generator humming alongside the cartoons playing on the black and white TV with bad aerial reception. There were about a dozen people there a few of whom ignored me completely like a ghost unseen. And equally a couple were so welcoming, friendly and giving it was truly touching. Still, this kind of situation was rarely comfortable, waiting and wondering what was happening. That's Indian time.

After a couple of hours of patient thumb twiddling the fire started to be prepared. A mound of logs and volcanic rocks stood four and half feet tall in front of a large dome tent like structure. Made of branch poles and interwoven blankets about fifteen feet in diameter and around five feet high, the fire pyre also now burned, heating the ancestral stones. Looking out into the foothills of the majestic Taos Mountain, land inhabited and owned entirely by that tribe of pueblo people, it had remained untouched for thousands of years. I wanted to go walking off into the mountain. It had an undeniable pull, beauty and magnetism—an urge I wanted to follow but my expressed thoughts were met with raised eyebrows and laughter.

"I grew up here, and I wouldn't dare," one of Des' cousins said. "There be Bruja's in them foothills. You'd never be seen again."

The bewitching pull quickly evaporated with the thought of being spirited away by some witchy medicine woman. I didn't need that again. So I sat and watched the fire burn for hours, heating the volcanic rocks to a glowing red mass. As the finishing touches were put into the lodge structure, one of Des' cousins exited the lodge with a glowing smile in his eyes, looking at me and saying loudly; "This a two door lodge—a clown lodge—too much power for just one door…we need another for the lightning to escape."

This was my first sweat and it was the real deal. I gathered it was going to be similar to an intense sauna in a dark womb like tented cave, a circle of song, healing, thanks and prayer. I was there to tend to my heart, my energetic pathways, and to better understand all that powerful lightning and electricity that had been building up within me. I still needed to hem my frayed edges, iron out the creases and folds that had crumpled my spirit many moons earlier.

Looking for guidance that would lead me safely over the bridge of myself, it had been beckoning there was no doubt. Having gone beyond physical peril, I knew there was a greater purpose I was being oiled for. Such intangible feelings were the most concrete aspects of my life and experience, the entire reason why I had chosen so much solitude and travel as my way. There were secrets and new directions, potent realities being revealed, and I was compelled to find and follow this lesser travelled way.

A real communion, the small prayer circle took us back before religion and into the dawn of ourselves, participating in a process unchanged for a long time. Just a small family inviting close friends and relatives to gather in a healing song and to do what they've done regularly for generations, in that same place for a thousand years, to sweat and sing, sing and sweat.

I learned that, shamefully, for much of the twentieth century it was illegal for any Native American songs, dances or ceremonies to take place punishable with prison and a $10,000 fine. There were many good reasons why Native American practices had gone underground. The government had them stalked like a golden eyed hawk, and staring back they fell deeper as prey.

Awakening with great fear they had known the hunt, the being hunted. Everything that was desired— their sense of value and worth was stolen. A wing clipped raven, the rug underfoot was pulled away.

Remembering the scowl in the eyes of the owl, behind solitude, desperation and desire for freedom, stood a dark cloak holding a sharp blade against their throats.

'We the People.'

Strange stories we heard back in those early days, it had all been seen and written. In the beginning was the word. Who heard and knew from whence it came? Understanding that was equal to the enigma of life herself. It was best to simply know oneself and discover the universe. The arrow had pierced the hand. Destiny had been made manifest. But we were playing life like a game of numbers, universal order a rolling dice. Balance at stake in the global account—at odds were emotions in the cycles of life. The only point was to fulfill a resourceful will. Letting go of loss and gain, there was only one number to find. The winning number. Simply one. How many times had the odds favored freedom? Timeless bidding lost and forgotten. Individuals had been imprisoned as numbers on the dice. Essence mined and source extracted, great consequence came with creation, perhaps Truth still could be a valuable gold.

The prophecies had been written and Earth herself was calling for understanding, a collective vision to avert the prophecies. For more than ten-thousand years from one generation to another they had been told of this time in which we were now living. It had been seen, written and remembered. And here we were, witness to the truth of our ancient selves living in the age we'd heard talked about since the first dawn. The 20th century's world wars had single handedly shaken the earth, twice. The 'Gourd of Ashes'—the atom bomb had exploded, even the structure of creation—the DNA spiral was uncovered and split. Strange stories they were to hear, back in those early days, but it had all been heard, seen and written. In the beginning was the word. Who knew where or really understood where it came from? Understanding that was only equal to understanding the enigma of life herself. Better to simply know thyself, and know the universe. Now nature was no longer in the hands of just the Almighty, but an almighty gift placed in our hands.

Ten-thousand years ago the stories of this far off future seemed so strange. So otherworldly. It had been passed down as part of the oral tradition, the prophecies recorded on stone tablets and given to the early peoples when they emerged from their ships after the deluge. Important records they were told to always keep safe. The white tribe of the North were given the teachings of lightning, the spark of life, the power of fire to ignite and move the world. The yellow tribe in the South were given the dominion of air, the understanding of breath and the technology of mind. The black tribe in the West were given the teachings of water, the greatest force and power to create sweeping change, and the red people in the East were given guardianship of the Earth.

Each of the four peoples who kept this sacred knowledge used the four colors to identify the teachings. The path of Rainbow Warriors—the whirling rainbow, the four worlds needed one another to create unity. The world would never be complete without the connection and presence of all four elements together. The wheel of prophecy and destiny still waited to be spun. The tablets all remained intact, revered and kept by their guardians in Kenya, Tibet, Hopi land, and Switzerland. It was even said that if you traveled through the earth from Hopi land you'd find yourself in Tibet. These nations reflected one another, the Hopi word for Sun and Tibetan word for Moon being the same, and vice versa, the Tibetan word for Sun was the Hopi word for Moon. Both peoples also loved turquoise and red coral and since the first dawn adorned their bodies with these stones as a conduit to remain connected with the timeless spirit of the teachings.

At the sweat lodge, the fire burned. The rocks glowed and the rain continued, not dampening the fire but making for an alchemical evening. As night fell we entered the lodge—our naked selves wrapped in just towels, moving into the darkness in an anti-clockwise direction, taking a seat inside the dark womb lodge by the fire pit. A very tight space, we were all huddled together in the darkness, knees touching earth or one another. As the songs were sung and prayers offered, the sweat beaded up on my scalp and started to seep from every pore. Each round of the ceremony, ten more glowing rocks were shoveled into the central pit. These enormous hot rocks were referred to as ancestors, the grandparents, the mineral origins forged in the fires of creation, holding the eternal flame.

The small lodge fit about a dozen of us, making ourselves as small as one could be. There was nowhere to move but inward in that searing sweaty womb. Voices and songs echoing, rocks popping and fire cracking, when it got so hot that it was simply too difficult to breath, I folded myself down deeper into the earth. Head between knees, myself in all manner of contortion to feel the cool earth and suck in air all while still giving thanks for being there. For many hours we sat in that circle, steaming and sweating in the scorching heat. Whittling my senses away, prayers of thanks and love flowed through me like the river of perspiration that seeped from my pores. Heartfelt appreciation made the process easier to submit to, the songs resounding and the drum pounding, sweet musky fragrances of cedar and juniper infusing the inner sanctum.

Between rounds of prayer, song, sweat and stones, there was the opportunity to exit and breathe in the chill fresh air. Gazing into the infinity of stars, the grasshoppers buzzed in the shamanic night. Between the fire and rain, native songs, prayer, and distant healing being sent out to loved ones far and wide, it was only natural to feel set aloft, full of light, giddy minded and carried away by Garuda into the infinite wish of the spiritual night.

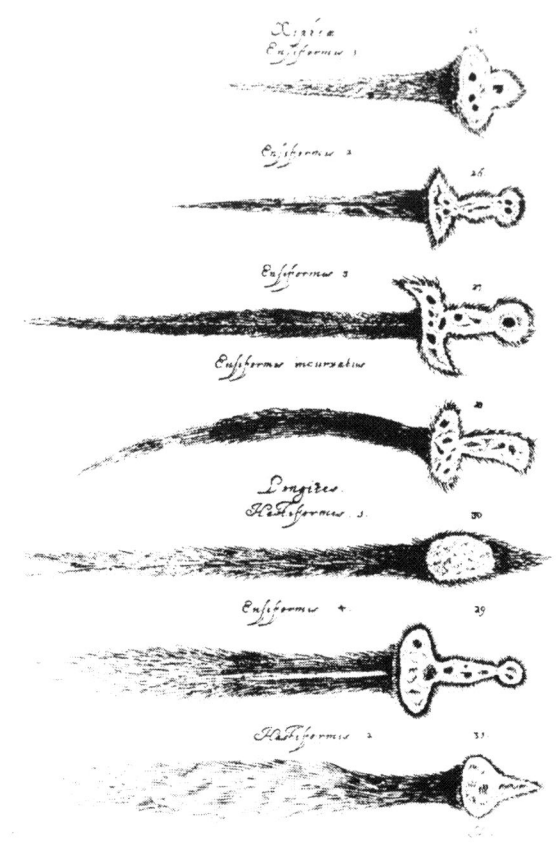

VI. Natural Mystic

Through December and into January 1996, ever restless and in search of the next unknown, the wanderlust of my inner quest had me by the short and curlies. I travelled on, leaving Des and his cousins, and headed north through the San Luis valley into the Sangre de Cristo Mountains.

I had met Shinay whilst hitch hiking. Dark haired with a constant smile that betrayed her bad teeth, her beauty wasn't surface but way deeper than skin, her generosity was both full and uncomplicated. Working for the Post Office and living on a piece of land with bare bones structures, she let travelers stay on her land—couch surfing without couches at ET village, as she called it—Earth Travelers village. She was fascinated by alien stories and the UFO activity. That was the trade—listening to stories of entities from the other side of the universe and doing a few chores—moving trash and building materials, and chopping wood.

I stayed in a yurt surrounded by trees on a hillside over-looking the valley. There were a couple of trailers on the adjoining property and an odd assortment of seekers and hippies who lived close by. I spent much of my time alone carving small pieces of stone, sitting in the sunlight on a log. Carving a piece of red pipe stone with a knife, shaping the soft stone, turning to look at it I started to see the form of a flat headed eagle emerge. Working with my hands and being really conscious of the energy of the stone, the blade and my hand, I found myself with a remarkable knack for it. I also seemed to have a natural talent for napping arrowheads out of obsidian with an antler—an old school craft that I took to like a fish to water.

Late that afternoon I was taking a walk surveying the forests and hills in the immediate area, and I climbed up onto a high point where I could peer down onto the five pointed skylight. The circular yurt planted there looked like a white spaceship glowing in the trees. At sunset the colors of the sky were shifting and from a larger hill behind the yurt I watched a small golden light—a ball of it, not fire but a small bright golden sphere, rising up into the sky. The strangest thing, there was nothing normal about it. Arcing upwards and over me, hovering above seemingly about the size of my fist just a few arms lengths away, It just ripped, up, up, up, tearing off into the deep night sky where it became just a distant blip perhaps on someone else's radar. Like some roving satellite barely visible in the starry sky I saw it up close and curious—and it was intelligent light, bright, not dim like you and me.

Later that evening a few hippy kids from adjoining properties—all around my age came to the yurt with Djembe and Egyptian drums. We all brought up wood for the fire—a stove heating the place from the winter chill. Sitting on straw bale bed furniture and log stumps around the hearth beneath the skylight, that night I heard about an upcoming equinox drum festival—a 'Rainbow Gathering' that was being planned. Long before the lions' rainbow was appropriated in the name of pride, the prismatic celestial banner called all the peoples together under one heart, one truth, one destination. Sexuality was only the tiniest part of it all, like this complicated little nothing of a blue sphere on the edge of the vast endless universe.

I had ridden the Edinburgh bacchanalia through to its tantric Javanese dimensions, and now that I'd been spat out the other side, what was important to me was personal understanding, sensitivity and soul compassion that went beyond the desires and fires of passion. Twenty-one young and ready to renounce the world, at the time, this ascetic path was essential to my burgeoning awareness, strengthening my vital energy, living rugged and rough. At times I craved the kindred companionship of a sexy soul mate, but I didn't meet too many gals that were on the same page. So I accepted my lot and choice, making a personal pact to venture as far as the cosmic conveyor belt was going to carry my burning heart.

That night in the yurt we played some ecstatic rhythms with drums and didgeridoo, passing the pipe that I had carved, marijuana never ending. Calling spirit down into the room with thanks for the rhythm of life and light, the molecules of cold air were infused by more than breath. Sound lifted us continuously higher and higher in waves, creating of that circular space a ship, a craft that was geared for lift off.

When the music eventually died down and the others drifted back to their abodes, I stocked the stove with wood, climbed into my sleeping bag cocoon, pulled multiple blankets over me and fell deep into lucid dream. Swiftly I found myself in a kind of school, a place of teachings and light, being given strange and specific knowledge involving geometry. I always did need extra help with math at school. Through overlapping concentric circles which turned into platonic solids, I travelled through the geometry of the elements digesting and becoming each before ascending into the next.

Earth, fire, air, water into the universal mind. From cube to tetrahedron, octahedron, icosahedron transformed within the dodecahedron, the composite

teachings becoming a multi-dimensional star craft, connecting lines of spinning light in constant movement. The spheres of the flower of life were an outer force field surrounding a crystal pointed star-chamber that enclosed my being in a radiant field. A light body— an etheric vehicle that would allow me to move through time and space was being shown to me. Traveling beyond the seven stars and four moons, these thirteen spheres were all one spirit. And they too were part of a larger spirit family which resonated, recycled and repeated all the way back through time. The seven rays all had an intelligence about them, each emanating a wave, a hue, a tone, a unique signature of astral light.

Upon awakening my eyes were filled with patterns, and in the cold morning air snug beneath my hoodie in my sleeping bag cocoon, I felt separated from my shell, my body, as though it were my core soul, my true self, not just my mind and body that was seeing now. A few words and names buzzed in my head. Mer ka ba. Flower of life. I lay there for a while thinking about the dream and feeling that soul sensation. The cool mist of morning in the uninsulated canvas yurt occupied the space, cajoling me to get the stove burning and brew some morning coffee.

Stepping outside beneath the trees in the morning light with my cup of coffee, I walked over to the clearing that overlooked the valley. A majestic eagle swooped and played in the winds. Flying closer, it came and hovered above me, staying there motionless as my eyes, mind and spirit reached upward. There was an inexplicable sense of connection between us, a silent conscious force, us both being the watcher and observed. It was quite a beautiful moment lasting just a few minutes, but long enough to be intriguing. My native friends would have said that it was a sign of my connection to spirit, the higher source. I just felt blessed with the opportunity to admire this majestic creature and feel the air beneath its wings.

Wandering on and catching a ride north, I headed to Manitou Springs a small town at the foot of Pikes Peak. It appealed to me for its arty nature and off beat way. The natural soda mineral springs dotted through the town each had a different taste, the park and town center that ran along the creek making it both welcoming and picturesque. The beginning of February and I'd been roaming around New Mexico and into Colorado for 6 months. I hadn't had any money for most of that, but I had found that my talent for making arrowheads and stringing together bits of jewelry and what not with the stones I found and traded seemed to serve me nicely in a barter. People were happy to trade some food or dry place to crash for one of my handcrafts. Once in a while I'd play my didge and put out a few magic bits and bobs of gems and stones I'd carved up, but I'd like to be off the beaten track mostly, so it kind of defeated the purpose though the little song I sung there with sounds and stones, seemed to bring all sorts of human grain out of the woodwork, like termites weaving their way to the light. Always interesting and interested, the people who'd find and approach me became quick friends, welcoming me all in, knowing that I was well out of place and time, a traveler living home free.

On the edge of a steeply inclined pine and evergreen forest leading up to the Pikes Peak, nearby was a tremendous place fittingly called the Garden of the Gods, and not far off was the Cave of the Winds, both places of great rock and spirit. With my hoodie, sleeveless Afghan coat that I'd been Christmas gifted by a kind stranger, sleeping bag and didge slung across my back, I headed off down creek to a small cave where I bedded down for the night. In the morning, making what could vaguely be described as music in the park by the river I met a Park Keeper who asked if I was playing for money. Knowing sometimes parkies and police didn't like buskers and all, which I wasn't, I said no I wasn't, I was playing to wake up and see what the day brings, which was in the fact the true story. Hearing my accent and all, he asked me where I was from and handed me a ten dollar bill. Wishing me well he walked away. Smiles all round, I went to the diner across the street and filled up on coffee and had a proper breakfast to set me right ahead. With a few dollars more still in my pocket, it was a whole other mindset not concerning myself with money but it was nice to have a few bucks. I had no credit card, phone or address. I hadn't even had to write my signature since the previous summer. I was just about as out there as I could've ever imagined.

"Where are you from?" What a question! At that point it was kind of hard to say. I'd been asked so many times, I felt like giving a new answer each time. But I wouldn't mess with good people too hard, though I watched it like a hawk. If I told them the place I was born, it could turn out to be like a trick and I'd get asked a million boring questions about how I got there, quickly becoming an interrogation, however interesting for the other, for me, not so much. I had to keep it in the moment, keep it real for myself. Or worse still I might have to listen to a yawn about someone or other's friend who once was in London studying, yada, yada, yada.

Sometimes I'd weave the hippie yarn, that it was about where I was at and not where I was from, mostly just to be a bit cheeky and flippant or whatever. But the best answer for the traveler on the endless road, was always the last place you came from, and questions about where you were going mostly evaded answer. That way I found I could be fully where I was at, free to discover what I may, welcomed as I would be or not. It was about being there in the landscape and magic with the freedom to go inward, be in the wilderness, in contact with some semblance of modern life, but still find some solace beyond the cushy edge of the contemporary world. It wasn't just me, the one with the social disease. Society herself was a sick puppy. The concrete juju and social disorder still lingered in my bones, all those years swimming in old world city waters and walking amongst soot covered stone with the ghosts of centuries past. Out there under the big sky of the American west, beyond the paved highways that rushed like lemmings to their fully articulated end I was seeking the rare, the unusual, a beautifully impossible potential of being. To just be. As if it was possible to discover a way to be apart but whole, self-sufficient but together as one, not having, needing or wanting. Just being.

I'd heard some say that all the problems of man came from him not being able to just sit quietly in a room and it was true, the business and busyness of man came from many unnecessary distractions. Politics and tricks, the system was a shit stem. Two thousand years of democracy and this was what we got. Pull the other one! I didn't get it and wasn't buying it. Having studied it deeply at the academic sausage factory that was called high school in Britain, I knew the schisms in the isms. Capital communed and you didn't have to be a rocket scientist in a secret mountain base to know the shit was going to blow. They even planned on it, grown children getting rich and getting a kick out of the breakdown of society. Short sighted, they knew not what they did. Like any true nut I wanted out of the white box. I didn't even want the room to sit quietly in. A casket or a boat of reeds? I wanted to be awake, alive not banging my head against the wall in my lonely room. If I was to be here, to really be here now, then I wanted to be close to the heart and soul of the world. That meant going into rarer elements and resources—the hidden ones, ones that come out only when needs must. I was at the source. She'd found me there those many moons earlier, capturing me into her spell. In the Goddess' sweet prison under the dome of the sky, I learned more and more each day about the movement of internal energy. The light that came from the deepest space within.

Learning valuable lessons in all kind of ways—I accessed my growing inter dimensional awareness, knowing that I had died that last summer. The laws of my life felt way different than before, having fallen into the abyss. Climbing out on the other side, I wondered where I truly was. Sleeping on the hard ground proved a good remedy and strangely comforting. Climbing into her when it was time to lay down and enter the dreamtime, I worked hard at making peace with that sacrifice of my comfort. I mined within for my purpose and gift, whittling away, surviving and thriving in the wilder regions of myself. I played for life, feeling safe and sound in heart, mind and body—at one and trusting.

I knew there were worse things than an uncomfortable night sleeping on hard earth and I valued the independence in it. Not paying rent, not being a guest, I was free—at home in the world regardless. No money, no money to worry about. Granted, my feet would get cold first, right at the darkest hour before dawn, so I learned to put on extra socks and wrap them in a blanket so I could sleep better. Early morning was always a good shakedown, my bones needing a good jump around to remedy the offset of night, the tweak and twist of it stretched out.

There was some method there in my madness. It was about finding my own rhythm, my natural pace from within. I was becoming limber and it was a good balance—the comfort and discomfort keeping me vital. Knowing the cold in my bones and being able to heat 'em up through my thoughts and stillness was a valuable skill. To be able to hold some peace through the night, alone in the cave of my mind. With the flickering flame and shadows on the wall, I tested my human and spiritual mettle, feeling the personal mission of it all. However wavering, beyond worry, I felt I had died many times and there was no need for fear. Something strange, bigger, even more beautiful was at work and I knew I was part of an essential wave that was building. I could feel it in my cells, the impulse of knowing thoughts guiding and directing me onwards.

The red hills had the invisible force of a whole other ancient population. Painted Earth, the deep red sandstones and oxides, the blood of man and the sacred ground were one. Somewhere in between, I emerged from my birth meteor, landing my light craft on the magical hill. Out there in Colorado, my home was like a path that sparkled in the stars and in the colors of the land. And I was in it, day and night. Slipped in between tones of earth and skin, humming and vibrating to resonate with the stone through every changing frame of light, night and day. My heart felt like a battery, a complex time machine deeply set, switched on, circuits and currents flowing as they opened to new sensations of being. At one in the earth temple of the world, being there, within it, the eye of the watcher and observed, I could see and hear all the echoes and reflections bouncing and bubbling up to the surface.

Manitou. At the end of Main Street across from the park and the river was a building which was operated as a healing center. I'd also heard that they had a flotation tank and having done a few sessions in Edinburgh, I wanted to check it out. I thought they might also have a shower and facilities, and after a few days of going commando I thought maybe I could do a trade to get a proper clean in. So I introduced myself. Luckily enough I met one of the owners, a motherly beauty named Rhonda her dark hair, sapphire blue eyes and warm smile completely disarming me, as she looked into my eyes and mind, and seemed to know where I was coming from instinctively.

A seer, psychic and healer, the place too had a vibrant and welcoming energy. Showing me around, Rhonda candidly confessed how this Victorian house was once an old time house of pleasure and giggled at how now the rooms were session rooms for alternative therapies. There was always a happy ending in store, but of a cosmic kind. Of course there was the flotation tank spa area. I felt so welcomed and at home and as if by the magic of my way was given a key and full use of the facilities and tank at night, when the place was not open for business. My friends back in those teenage years of early imagining always did call me jammy—a jammy bastard, which meant lucky, but I didn't believe in luck. I knew what I was giving and receiving, even if it came in unexpected ways. Magic was simply love and energy combined.

So on the nights when I hadn't been hanging with new friends at the bar listening to music and the weather was a bit inclement for a hike into the hills to camp for the night, I'd head to the healing house, use my open invitation and enter through the backdoor, shower up and sleep on a massage table, or slip into the flotation tank. At first I began with around two hours of deep submersion sleep, feeling my body align, weightless in the dark warm wet space. As I became more and more comfortable with it, and the more friends and invitations I found in town, I began to spend longer periods inside the tank when I did sleep there. Sometimes four or six hours I'd spend in the windowless chamber, deeply immersed in the liquid unconscious. I'd feel the warmth of the weightless sleep deep in my body, freeing my mind. Being able to move and float, stretch in the water and find my tensions and tendons release, the twinges and tweaks still pulsed through my right hand but found a more forgiving tone from the outdoor winter life I'd been leading.

Letting go of what I held onto in the muscle knots and scar tissue of my right hand, I was refining my internal energy. Growing in leaps and bounds, becoming stronger and able, my hand felt so different from six months of fire making, stone carving and living rough. I'd been working a lot with gemstones and I had a good little collection going of my hand made obsidian arrowheads, soapstone pipes, many colored opals, tiger's eye—a couple of them keeping a watch, various colored quartz, kyanite and even a really crazy seven inch wand of a Peruvian star seed crystal. I kept them all with me inside this pouch I had traded—a medicine pouch made of a turtle shell, handcrafted and lined with suede by one of Des' cousins in the Pueblo.

I was learning to use the stones to move energy when my arm and body would twinge with pierces and aches, keeping the energy through my shoulder, elbow and hand of my right arm pulsing and flowing. Performing adjustments to my left side where I overcompensated in balance, it was kind of profound being able to feel and move the subtle energies through my body. Even to be able to recognize the connection between my limbs— my creative and receptive, to even be able to feel the interaction and relationship between my right palm and left heel.

The stones became like magical friends, guides that I learned to listen to. They had much that they could teach me. The deeper I tuned in the more I could hear and see their true quality, value and nature. They held secrets of transformation, in the same way that birds flew and flowers grew. Energy flowing where my attention was going, some people could communicate with plants and animals, and I could hear gemstones. It was a simple magnetic understanding and electrical synaptic impulse—perhaps it was like Java, a programming language that had been encoded within me. I could see the pitfalls of using this 'power' for one's own seductive pleasure. Touch had its own magically addictive grip. Though I could feel the power coursing through me, I never thought that it was my point or purpose. All of these things, these subtle motions of energy connected with my emotions. Attachment to reason, matter, substance: letting go of concepts with a greater force of light and mind; that was the way forward. Suspension of disbelief was more than a concept—it had been a gift. It allowed me to see and experience places and people I would never have otherwise encountered, being pulled fully into the picture. There was in fact method in my madness, not that anyone else might have known.

It wasn't for anyone else. This was my trip, and what a long strange one it had indeed been. I noticed details instinctively. Branches and roots, human and animal tracks, I still looked for direction in signs and omens—

sometimes even hour to hour wondering which way to go next. Wanderlust had no problem with getting lost. How could you find yourself if you never got lost? I had no worries, nor fears. I had chosen my sacrifices and it was as if the universe conspired in my favor, pulling me into the slipstream of magical consciousness. Wakefulness and dream crossed into one another. I'd seen Coyote, Wolves, Deer, Elk, Antelope, Buffalo, Magpies, Crows, Hawks, Vultures, Eagles, and even numbers—repeating numbers, and names, the coincidence of connection was seamless. Everything showed me something, if not only itself. As King Lear in the wilderness knew, this way madness lay.

Manitou Springs had long been renowned for esoteric arts, the occult even being outlawed there in the 1970s when the town boasted more covens of witchcraft than anywhere else in the US. Not that I was into pagan covens, witchcraft or anything, though I did have a basic understanding, recognizing its symbolism, but I was very wary of manipulation of forces and those who practiced that kind of magick. Somehow earth magic, colour consciousness, and healing, felt like an entirely different plane. Sure there were spells and amulets, ancient mantras that came from sacred traditions, used to hone in on energies and qualities that promoted transformation, but one had to be sure and careful, knowing that the forces were often more powerful than our true understanding of them, and repercussions would be had, one way or another.

The sense of being connected to a higher force was indeed intoxicating, and quiet communion with the spirits that seemed to guide me was what kept me on track.

Late one afternoon, I'd been hiking around in the Garden of the Gods and I sat and played my didge to an audience of twelve inquisitive deer and one swooping red hawk, when a fellow wanderer appeared. He looked like he'd been living rough, wide eyed and peaceful as he was. Approaching, he sat and listened with me. After a while immersed in the deeply transporting sound waves, I stopped playing and we started chatting. He had been collecting arrowheads—old ones he'd find scattered and hidden from the last century. He had quite a knack for it. He said he could hear them, a high pitch calling would draw him to the point, sometimes deeply buried, digging instinctually like a dog he'd always come up trumps. I showed him some of my own made obsidian points I'd napped with an antler, yet he knew that they were newly made. They were too perfect he said.

We walked around the Garden of the Gods there together, him telling me the native names of the red sandstone monoliths that towered all around us, rising erect from the valley floor. Carved by a cosmic hand of wind and time to appear like native giant, these totems of red earth and spirit gave the place its fitting name. Two hundred foot tall chiseled faces of regal chiefs, native women and children could be seen clear as day in the rock, the twilight shadow giving the hard stone an other-worldly presence. It was said that the sandstorms created the rock spirits in the same way that experience created character in human beings.

We sat on a rock watching the sun set, as the night encroached we started to hear the strangest ticking sound coming from the enormous rock directly behind us in the calm quiet night. It was odd, the sound of a ticking clock echoing through a stone chamber. My imagination ran wild with speculation, but nothing made sense and I had to investigate it.

The rock face behind me was about around fifteen feet tall to the first ledge and opening into the rock structure that couldn't be seen from the ground. I was fired up, compelled, and in that indigo dusk all of a sudden I was climbing the vertical rock face, finding foot and hand holds easily in the swiftly swooping darkness. The sound was compelling, even though climbing in darkness was stupid at best, especially with my history, it simply couldn't be avoided. I was possessed by the sound, moving through me, like I was climbing into a ventricle of my own heart. A physical imperative, nervous energy and impetuousness combined, I pulled myself up and over, onto the ledge.

Two trees stood behind that front rock face in a narrow gully high up inside the rock, roots breaking upwards through the crumbling red rock, hugging the rocks for dear life as they twisted and climbed. Ever reaching for the sky, against the odds water was drawn from deep below. Beyond the two trees at the end of the gully incline was an opening that created a picture window looking out to a majestic towering Indian chief of a giant rock.

As I approached the trees the sound of the tick-tocking got louder, reverberating through me. Instinctively reaching out with my left hand against the bark of the left cottonwood tree, and stepping my right foot off the roots of the right tree, I followed suit with my right hand and other foot. The sound of the pulse and its heart beat now rushed through my body, both trees had a pulse and they beat together like a damn metronome. I'd never heard or imagined anything like it—the echo of the life force of the trees in unison, singing out through me in that stone chamber.

Straddling those trees, legs and arms splayed it was a tremendous surge in energy that I felt pulsing though me and yet another dose of crazy experience for which I had no road map. Letting go of the bark, and stepping off the roots onto the rock, I climbed the incline, putting my hands on the rock either side of me as I stood out looking at the stone structures rising up from the valley floor in the fallen night. Man I felt thankful. In fact so much, that I started to speak out loud to the Sky and the Earth and to Spirit. Making a prayer, it was my statement of gratitude for the keys to the rare and sacred world I had been given. The words tumbled through me, my heart exploding with love and thanks, fathoming the infinite possibilities and potent secrets to which I was for privy. And then, even more unbelievably so, the hugest, brightest shooting star or whatever it was, shot into view perfectly framed by the rock window. A beaming golden bright white light it swiftly streaked into orbit before being extinguished into the earth.

VII. Riding the Snake

*March 22nd-25th 1996. Pikes Peak National forest.
Elevation 10,000 ft.*

A small gathering was forming, a drum circle and
rainbow festival that had been whispered on the wind.
A word of mouth happening for nomads, rainbow family
and outdoors lovers high in the mountains for the spring
equinox, a comet was coming. We had heard about it
on the radio, Comet Hyukatake named after a Japanese
comet hunter whose name meant '100 samurai.' It wasn't
that odd how the comet sparked significant excitement,
we never got much advance warning, and all of a sudden
these Messengers were there, certain trajectory unknown,
with messages from beyond our universe, and the water
that brought life to Earth. It was a personal encounter
that could affect consciousness on a large scale, even
bring about total destruction or everlasting change. No
one really knew. And for those of us who were connected

to the natural world, the cycles of nature and planetary pulse, the energy of it felt strong. Even hearing about it or talking about it seemed to enliven me and my friends, feeling as though we were going to have a rare close encounter on its blazing path through our stratosphere.

Rocking up scooby doo style in their camper van, Tom, Jade and their nine month old baby Patience unloaded and locked up. I'd met them down in Manitou, becoming fast friends, they were always so generous sharing food, company, good times and the occasional night on their sofa given inclement weather. We'd gathered supplies and gear and headed to the mountains to be in the great outdoors for the equinox, the comet and drum festival. Big skies in the Rocky Mountains went on forever. The rhythm of drums echoed playfully on the chilled winds. People of all ages were parking, camping and getting situated. About a hundred people had gathered there for the long weekend, an open hearted warm vibe infused everyone. One group had been camped there for a week already and had built a wooden structure for their outdoor kitchen next to an open clearing. The kettle was on the grate over the fire. Tarps made a roof beneath the trees. I walked on by, keeping a distance as I headed to the ridge surrounding the open clearing. "Welcome home bro" shouted one of the group—a young dude sitting there drinking a cup of tea.

Welcome home! Nowhere man, now here, I Am.

Walking through the open clearing and up the back onto a ridge, I wove my way through various well hidden camp dwellings, watching people put up shelters and tents. Folks were friendly, busy building their domains. I did meet a mystic man in his fifties with a silver beard and an Afghan hat named Rod. I was curious, because he was hard at work building himself an Igloo, packing snow, making ice blocks by hand and doing it all so swiftly and expertly. Not having a tent, I was looking for a rock shelter or place I could construct a simple bivouac out of branches for a safe warm dry spot where I might lay down my drop sheet and climb into my sleeping bag when the hour came. An Igloo seemed a bit out of my element, but I was nevertheless impressed by his wherewithal. Talking for a few minutes, he pointed me up the way, saying there was a spot for me over that away,

"You'll know it when you find it, just follow the natural flow of the land."

So I walked a little way jumping from rocks, through snow and grass, up and across until I found a small path that'd been carefully lined with stones. It seemed like it'd been there a long time, and led to the entrance of a make-shift shelter. Huge teepee branch poles were interwoven with blankets and tarps that leaned against a large upright slab of rock. I scoped the perimeter and up close and there were no traces of inhabitants around this most excellent lodge. It seemed uncanny, why would someone leave such a perfect intact dwelling? I called in but the sound kind of whispered back, bouncing off the stone wall. It was empty, but the light that funneled through the fire pit chimney opening hummed, changing pitch as late afternoon light in the high mountain air could only do.

The fire pit inside looked cold and dormant but when I stirred the ashes with a stick, a little dry tinder fell in from the rocks around the edge. Surprised again to see glowing embers, they got brighter and ignited as I stared at them, fanning them with my hand and placing some more dry leaves into the small fire pit. This was an Indian fire, not a white man fire. You could tell by the size of the small pit. Earth people always made small fires, making them last, building the heat within slowly and surely. In contrast white men liked to make massive fires, big, fast and bright, inevitably running out of fuel on the long cold night. We all had something to learn.

Welcome home, the flame is always burning.

Setting down my sleeping bag, ground sheet and poncho, I took off my didgeridoo that was slung over my shoulder and squatting, placed it to me lips, a deep vibratory sound starting to form. The particles of light streamed in and the smoke leaving the space danced in the deep resonant sound. I was psyched to have found such a sweet spot. Pure magic. I'd been wandering for about 7 months though New Mexico into Colorado, staying in caves by hot springs, camping out in forests, trailers and teepees, thanks to the kindness of friends and strangers along the way. Not all who wander are lost. Still relearning to use my right hand again, I had made the effort to get off the grid, off the reservation of contemporary society, its corporations, rules and regulations. I liked being an invisible one. Compared to the contemporary tabloid culture I came from, it was freeing. No mirrors hanging on my walls, having no walls, I started to understand the world as a reflection of myself. Living beyond the confines of my own perception, I could see the underlying shapes of things. Living outback of the modern world, time took on a whole new presence beyond clocks, watches and appliances. It was so obvious and different from my breeding, my education, my molding and it was comforting. After the accident, I was devastated internally. Rhythms shot, the best call of action seemed to be to go deep, and listen to my dreams wherever I might find them.

Welcomed warmly as foreigners in distant lands so often are, the ground embraced me, speaking my language in secret tongues. The expanse of nature and sky was an opportunity to explore the source of my thoughts, heart and life.

Far, far away from the concrete worlds and material illusions of my home cities, the rising consciousness of the age, a collective awakening of otherworldly proportions was reaching its millennial crescendo. Beyond the Pulp Fictions and Nirvana suicides, OJ smokescreens and the US's non meeting of Kyoto Environmental protocols, beyond the urban sprawl and fast food highways that all defined the surface of life in the '90s, there were still higher intelligences at work, being tapped into by more than a few of us.

A new time was dawning and there were many wake up calls and messages being sent and received pre cell phone and Internet. The coming of the tribes, the uniting of the peoples of the four races of Earth, the children of the Whirling Rainbow were gathering as it had been written.

People of all ages gathered and made themselves at home, strangers becoming fast friends amongst the many camp fire satellites dotted around the mountainside like constellations. Occupying a large swath of land the gathering was spread out and you could hear the circles of drums syncopating from every direction through the wind and the trees.

Seated with Rod, Tom, Jade, Patience, and Andrew Appleseed. Andrew was a dude in his late 20^s with long hair, who looked like a writer or at least a thinker. You can tell those types, they always look like they are having a parallel thought, dust and vapor, aware of being both the watcher and observed. Huggy Bear was there too. Impulsive, short, bearded, round and layered in clothing. A couple of decades older than me, he seemed constantly euphoric, positive outlook oozing all over the place. Beautiful Ishara also sat with us with her son Mars, her four year old cougar cub. Sharing food made over the campfire, we laughed and drank plenty of tea, mixing lemon and a few wee drams of whisky just to round it out nicely.

I learned that there were some people who had been staying in the hogan, but had left a few days earlier. It was on the vortex of the hill, the spot where the energy paths and leylines crossed over. Rod, Huggy Bear and Andrew had been talking about it all. Pulling out a green malachite claw from the Turtle shell pouch strapped to my belt, I gave it to Mars who had been climbing around on my didge. It reminded me of him, and thought he'd like it. Mesmerized, he took it over to his mother Ishara and relaxed into her lap, transfixed and playing with the claw, his blue eyes bright and wide.

Intrigued by the didgeridoo, I told them the story of where it came from, in the dreamtime, and how coming home at dusk a warrior had seen a dead branch lying on the ground, when he picked it up, he saw daylight coming in the other end and noticed there were a lot of little insects in there. He blew through it to get rid of them and the termites blew into the air, all becoming the stars. The sound made the stars shine, glimmering paths of light, particles forming waves in lines of light. For thousands of years people were drawn to the sound and had painted their bodies with colored ochre and danced to its rhythm. As the old story went, it was said that when the warrior died, his spirit left his body and went into the hollow log so it could travel along the song lines, back home to its place amongst the stars.

I could've just told them I got the didgeridoo from an Australian dude who had a market stall in Edinburgh, but the story of the song lines was better, and also true.

Transfixed, watching the sky and resting by the fire, the samurai comet was getting surely closer to Earth arcing through the atmosphere with its white starry light and ever growing green and blue tails. As I played the didge, the sound seemed to magnetize our attention and the intensity of the comet's rays. Zoned out into the sound, it felt like it was traveling through the didgeridoo. I was tuning in, wakefully dreaming myself into the path of the comet. As the sound faded, the comet kept heading towards its close encounter, and it felt like the light at the end of the tunnel was both our destiny and fate.

As my new friends sloped off into the night or passed out by the fire light I pulled myself and possessions together from the sound trance and made my way back to my camp spot. The air was chilled and crisp, still plenty of snow on the ground in the tree shade. The hogan cold and empty was full of its own light. Still and quiet, the fire embers never needed a match to get going, just a stir of the ashes, fresh kindling and small pieces of dry wood worked their magic every time.

A dream spot, most peculiarly, or not in my out there experience, I had the same dream every night right there. More than lucid, it felt real like a visitation that kept returning. Maybe I was the visitor, or at least the guest. As I climbed inside my sleeping bag cocoon each night I'd quickly pass into netherworlds finding myself inside a drum, beneath the skin. A native woman sang hauntingly in repeating rhythm, banging the drum, chanting and wailing, and I was inside her song, inside her dream, beneath her skin, beneath my eyelids, inside the drum. The heart beat and beat inside the earth mother's womb, inside the dream, the place, the song and I and her indistinguishable. I felt the One, the All, her eyes cast over me in their protective and loving way.

In my cocoon I saw myself being sealed in lead, cast into a river, consumed into a living tree and cut apart. Rising up from my body and hovering over me, I felt wind resist against my arms as they became giant outstretched wings.

"Set the children free," I heard, ringing in my waking thoughts as I lay there looking up out of my hoodie in my sleeping bag cocoon, watching the morning light buzzing all around me. Above me the light seeped in against the granite rock slab that the branch poles, blankets and tarps used as their foundation wall. Morning light crystalized in an energetic and momentary still form, creating the Om.

I watched it dissipate before I unzipped, and when I sat up dozens of small polished pieces of amethyst crystals fell all around me. Laying on my chest beneath the zipped sleeping bag, I picked them up and looked at them closely, their purple heart shimmering with violet flame. Reaching out I grabbed my turtle shell pouch, gathering up the gemstones, herbs and amulets laid out on the suede next to it. I wrapped them up in the suede with the amethyst and placed them inside the turtle pouch.

Sleeping rough, this was my way of making any given place my sanctuary. Through these mysterious objects, talismans and amulets I felt a connection to friends, family, my thoughts and feelings, and every night before passing out, I'd give thanks, preparing my sanctuary and making this my daily ritual in an otherwise routineless life.

Putting jeans and boots on, the turtle pouch attached to my belt tucked away from sight beneath my hoodie and poncho, I headed out into the fresh cool morning. Looking up, the comet was still blazing its way through the early light, its silver streak stretching across half of the sky. Stretching my body, shaking myself out from the cold night, I sat by a fire with a few friendly folks who offered me a cup of coffee. A gal with blonde dreads was playing and singing Bob Marley's 'redemption song' on her guitar as other voices rang in with the known words.

"Emancipate yourselves from mental slavery; None but ourselves can free our mind. Have no fear for atomic energy, 'Cause none of them can stop the time."

I sat and shared with them a few early morning smiles—the waking blessing of the day, before sloping off into a light kissed clearing in the trees. Finding a trickle ice melt I took off my sweater and t-shirt, shoes and socks, and cleansed myself with the cold water, as I kept on singing with Bob Marley, like a conversation with a good friend in my head.

"How long shall we kill our prophets, while we stand aside and look? Yes, some say it's just a part of it: we've got to fulfill the book. Won't you have to sing this song of freedom?"

With eyes closed, I saw a violet light on the inside of me lids, sunshine feasting on my face, morning prisms in my eyes. "Free the children" I heard again, like a beat, looking for a song, and I saw a glowing figure in white inside of this violet light. Opening my eyes, I pursued this glimmer of a vision with some of my monkey magic movement practice, combining tai chi, yoga and my own form of martial art like a dancing fool on the hill. Where I came from, there was a legacy and heritage of fools on the hill. Beneath the trees in the sunlight everything felt a bit brighter, surer, stronger, more illuminating.

Meanwhile there was a big sweat preparing, a comet cleansing being conducted by a couple of clowns. There were a lot of people there, and many wanted in, but two dozen souls were going to huddle into the large dark womb lodge later that night for a close encounter with their own cometary nature. Having gathered large volcanic rocks throughout the day from the rocky mountainside, these were the ancient ones, the fire stones. These ancestors were the most important players, the key to the sweat lodge, and it wasn't like any old rock would do. They had to be volcanic for starters, otherwise the heat of the fire in which they'd be immersed would make them explode. They also had to be of a certain spirit- they'd have the mark of time, the cross of the ages. Hard to define, you'd know it when you saw it, because the rock would cry out: pick me, pick me, keen to heat things up and return to the source.

The lodge constructed in the traditional manner with branch poles and blankets, I found a natural bowl in the forest and had prepared some cedar and sage herbs to bless the fire stones and infuse the lodge with sweetness to please the spirits, like I'd seen and learned with Des and his cousins. Many wanted to experience the ceremony and having done a serious sweat just a couple of moons earlier I wasn't planning on being in it, just was happy to help set it up, powerful and special occasion as it was, comet and all.

The hogan—the spot where I was sleeping—was used as the impromptu center, a sacred center for the inner circle which I found myself a part. Not surprisingly it became the perfect setting for the most unexpected of secret ceremonies. With six of us sitting in there we'd all eaten one mushroom, given to us by Huggy Bear.

It was a large golden one with a long stem and a big cap, each one strangely and amusingly resembling the person to whom it was given, perfectly proportioned in shape and size.

Now streaking across the entire sky with its blue green tail, the comet really was a wonder dragon wrapping the whole earth and solar system up in in her tail. Ouroborous, it was a gift and we were all wrapped up. Inside the hogan, looking into the fire and listening to the drums, one of the flames started dancing and a tiny Goddess figure appeared before my eyes, a tiny dancer in the white hot flame. I knew then the mushroom was kicking in. The rhythm intensified and with it our small group started to hear one another's thoughts. We all knew it. Then someone new entered the hogan, wearing a top hat. This cat in the hat in full soliloquy took a seat without missing a beat telling a story that captured all of our attention. It wasn't even what he said, but what wasn't being said, what could be heard and seen in the silent worlds within. Speech was secondary, there was a primal communication at work in our psychic silence, language of the birds, the Green Language was the dust beside the vapor.

The movement of all essence and life greater than time. Forever bound to its cycles of change, the before and hereafter are measured and molded. Playground Earth's building blocks. Light and life create form and structure. A prospecting alchemist sees metaphysical gold in an obsidian mirror. Something ancient is remembered anew, as if for the first time. The map is drawn through intuition, in the heart of a clear minds' eye.

A lightning flash of inspiration, original and unique, never repeats. The moment is captured, like a spell. Art. Undying. Charged, mystically forged, manifest with a simple twist of fate, an act and movement in measures' mind. Is it the fullness or the emptiness that has value? The wasteland of the imperfect future whittles us back into a sensory void. Self-extinction and the building blocks of spirit. Touch the fabric of the illusion, the rock wall of the cave. Register the encounter with form, traveling back and forward in time. Hear the voice that harkens the early light. Move amidst the flickering fire, the shimmering reflection within the inner sanctum of self. Remember the green light of dawn approaches. Her name is Kismet.

So familiar, it was uncanny. Our silent thoughts reverberated with one another on the journey, each identifying a part to be played. Every circle of drums across the gathering now started to synchronize: the sweat lodge rhythms, songs and dancers. Thirteen circles drawn and connected by invisible lines, the hogan became the star tetrahedron at the center of the world, the axis mundi. Sitting cross legged I had to adjust my position and as I did, the slightest movement of muscles or wiggling toes shifted the rhythm. So sensitive, the flutter of a butterfly's wings could shift a world's fate. "My inner voice was telling me, Just trust, let go, we are all here, we are all related," and I felt so consumed that I understood how important every little thing was.

In that next instance I became what best could be described as a trance channel. Energy moved through me in quantum leaps, a spirit entering and overcoming me, forcing my left leg to rise up into the air, spirit writhing and riding within me like a serpent. I was completely aware, awake, not like you'd suspect, that I'd be blacked out in the process. No, I was fully stocked, conscious and I played my part to ride that crazy comet night as best I could.

One hundred Samurai indeed. Next thing I knew, I was picked up and hurled down to become like a rock in the fire pit, huddled into a ball. My conscious mind wide awake, I told myself to trust, to breathe, and as I did I became one with the Ancestors, climbing inside one of the volcanic rocks unearthed for the sweat lodge happening in parallel. Intimately connected, I was a little puckered tobe in some kind of psychic communication with the hot rocks, the fire stones throbbing in the sweat.

I told myself to trust, to keep trusting and breathing as I balled up in the small pit of the eternal fire. In the heart of the white fire, I was ablaze but not burning. The rock of ages, one of the Elders, that bore the mark of elemental initiation. As seismic cataclysms forced the hand of evolution, the bedrock of life on Earth, the glowing embers of lava consciousness grew brighter within the secret ceremony. Molten realizations solidified within the drumbeat and song.

Improbable as it sounds, but ain't it all—the next moment had me hugging the rock, holding on as I moved through space in what seemed like infinite velocity and ferocious stillness, holding on with faith, trust and seeing dear life after life as I rode that icy comet. From a burning rock to a fireball, the white heat cooled to white light, rock shrouded in gas and layers of ice. Riding that comet with all of my heart and all of my might, I saw his story, the comet's journey as it traveled across the universe since its cataclysmic inception. An imprisoned force, one of Saturn's children had been set free.

Ancient wanderer, I saw the oceans rise and recede, first man and woman emerging from giant Turtle ships. Making bricks of clay and planting seeds in the desert earth, the trees, children and villages all grew over many seasons and vast ranges. I saw this all wiped away in deluge, disaster and constant change. And the comet's tail reached so far behind me, traveling for what looked like aeons past, it wrapped it self round the world like the cosmic dragon that it truly was. Gripping my hold on that fiery ice ball, I watched seven generations go through their cycle of life. Death and rebirth, lives of constant work from dawn to dusk, moon to moon, year to year, lifetime after lifetime, seven times.

Mud of the Earth, bark of the tree, bud of the leaves, light of the sky. The roots of the lightning tree crossed the dreamtime, back from the origin, the source. Sending light to Earth to set the children free. A dazzling light poured onto the world, brightly illuminated clouds of protons hurled throughout the solar system rained down on Earth. Seven times stronger than the light of the Sun, so brilliant, even the Source of life was overpowered in the luminosity. In that primal wave I watched the celestial bodies dance. During a close approach to Jupiter, Saturn became unstable, exploded, and flared into a nova leaving only a fraction of its former self. Much of the matter was thrown off into space and greatly reduced in size, Saturn removed to a distant orbit. I saw rays and spokes intermittent and dark, as those of a wheel turning in streams of fire. The universal glory flamed in torches lighting up the land and I with a comet's eye view watched the planets turn from the cataclysm, renewing the life force on Earth.

Was this a past or future universal deluge I was seeing whilst suspended in animation on that comet?

The Satya Yuga, Sanskrit texts had scribed that many suns shone just before the deluge and being ignited, all of a sudden, the entire terrestrial sphere blazed forth and twelve suns shone with dazzling radiance that consumed the world. In that early age of celestial war, Saturn ruled over the planets in its fiery procession, unforgiving. Dark universal days, Jupiter took the reins of the celestial chariot, breaking Saturn apart and releasing the children to become wanderers with that ancient cosmic spark. Star seeds. The comet on a long haul through space time, its tail shone brighter, was longer and drew closer than for centuries we had seen.

Tumbling and turning, the rock of time counted on the Seventh generation. Forged in fire and water, taught alchemy and shown protective spells, even given the power to shake the world, we had climbed on the dragon's back, riding the snake in a great leap of faith. Looking towards a cosmic collaboration, the guiding light of the Goddess, ruled our terrestrial elements. Earth, Air, Fire and Water. The force of her astral fire, the radiation of her eternal flame seared away all obstacles for a whole new sphere of life's possibility. And in this incendiary light, I watched as the Turtle mothership emerged from the starry waters with its thirteen hexagram shields that formed its shell. The oceans rose over the planet and the giant turtle took to the sky waters, followed and surrounded by hundreds of thousands of its turtle clan babies. Each a soul swimming from the Source, the Origin, set free to begin anew, a new world, navigating the ocean by underwater mountains, currents, the winds and stars. And then I was inside the Great Earth Turtle looking into her eyes. Yes, Her. And we were the only two people on Earth.

The back gate of the Turtle was like a giant cargo ship, and inside of the ship was a holographic projection—a template of memory, time and evolution. A reincarnation machine, it showed us the formation of the world as choices were made and destinies fulfilled. Mapping light, time and space, in that chamber we were guided through color fields without moving. In stillness and motion through fields of soul memory, we were remembering what it was to be fulfilled, find love and purpose in the process.

We knew that we'd have to leave the Turtle's cosmic womb, taking life as individuals and splitting ourselves into many rays to set the light of time, and the children free. Many imprisoned souls remained enslaved by the dark oppressive forces of tyrannical planetary law from the first age. They knew not the difference between servitude and freedom anymore, debt was credit and war was peace. Looking into one another's eyes we knew in the aeon ahead we could only but love one another, being one, but that we would have to dissolve into the new world tested by the magnetic fields of earth.

Taught to forget through successive lifetimes and changing personifications of ourselves, we knew our awareness as a whole omnipotent being would be tested, and we would forget until we met each other on the way again. That's why we had planned to meet again. How could we not?

The spark of those ancient memories would happen all too sporadically for millennia. All these things we knew and still we would be tested against remembering ourselves. An ancient plan set out by a higher universal strategic force. We knew we had the power to remember and create enough emanations of ourselves until all possibilities were played out. Only self-realization remained free from the body of time.

As the oceans evaporated we saw many of the turtles become the boat people who survived the dreamtime crossing in their Turtle ships. Many had been washed asunder, turned to stone, becoming rocks in collision with mountains and waves. Lodged in cliffs and knocked to the ocean bed, still tens of thousands survived, finding themselves in the Pacific islands and throughout Meso America, the ancient founders of earlier civilizations. In the early days they retained memory of their Origin, having the powerful ability to move matter with mind, despite being a race of little ones. Lifting and moving giant rocks into places with ease using their knowledge of sound and vibration. When their time and work was done their spirits returned to their home far out in the universe, another star system with older more advanced technology and understanding.

The stones moved and molded were created as interstellar passageways, multi-dimensional doorways and the knowledge of their keys still remained hidden in the ancient tablets given through the four mountain doorways. Coming from the early light, the tablets of the Rainbow warriors, the Sundancers, the followers of the light were the original people given the prophecy of this time in which we lived. It had been written. Word up, but who was really listening? The Red, Black, White and Yellow tribes of the whirling rainbow saw that it was us. We were the first time travelers, remembering ourselves back when the first spoke in the wheel turned. Only a few got a glimpse of these other worldly elements at work. Drawing great feeling from afar and bringing that light to Earth, this was our human calling.

The cry for the lost tribes to come together could be heard on the winds. Spirit Eagles aligned, their arrows at the ready, thirteen arrows in their talons released from the moon, direction set for emancipations flight. Obsidian arrows with eagle feathered flight were shot forth so far that they were now returning again. And because the Arrow was still, the world was not yet destroyed.

Sunbathing on the moon, gazing at the golden wheel of the sun, I came round. Pulling myself back from the ball I was still curled up in, my eyes focused in the dark shimmering heat of the comet ceremony. I was feeling a bit toasty, but not burnt, my senses a little crispy from my cosmic collision with destiny. Acting out a role in a cosmic drama, the message and messenger were the medium. Who knew?! A few did. And a few others out there saw the shift. They were all on board in spirit, playing their part in our syncopated rhythms. You who know who you are. The serpent had risen and the rainbow whirled, it was a time for giving thanks, making offerings for the challenges ahead. The prophecy of the return of the winged serpent was being fulfilled, understanding and power rising within the collective imagination and consciousness of our generation.

At the end of the ceremony, Judah, the master drummer and black sun who guided and tempered the rolling thunder and giant waves of cosmic radiation, came in and took a seat on a rock as though it were a throne, not his own, but happily known that wherever he was, was indeed his seat of power. The story had been carried by the drums on the wind, the gift of communication, by the mighty tide. With the rhythm of water, it was seen that the lion tribe had and would create sweeping change, challenge equality, get to the heart of darkness, repair what had been torn away to spearhead a way into the future, the red green and gold prophecy, through its resistant twists and turns was still set towards unity.

A gift from the Earth, I handed Judah a peace of pipestone I had been given and carved along the way. It was a special piece I was told, as it had seven black marks, black stars that signified marks of spirit and looked like magic freckles in red stone. It was just my intuition that made me give him the pipestone, the stone that gave the Native people the power to communicate with Great Spirit, the migratory temple, meant to guide and keep a people in constant connection to source. The infectious spirit of the night bubbled over, and more and more people started to crowd into the hogan. Humming with excitement and warmth, everyone brought hugs and gifts, and I was presented with a pair of knitted gloves. A perfect gift all things considered, having everything, needing nothing, I was ready to give it all—my amulets, talismans and small possessions away. Still I was touched by the gloves, a simple practical gift that would keep my fingers warm and protected. Having taken the reins in the ride of my life, I was truly thankful.

Making my way out, I felt embraced and surprised at the sapphire blue light of the early dawn and the many, many hours of the long dark night that had passed. The sky still had its streaks of blue green glory, the trace of the passing comet etched an opening, showing the gateways of past and future, zipping a line of light across the arc of the huge Rocky Mountain sky. Sitting out there relaxed, under the early dawn sky, stretched out and leaning against a tree was Andrew Appleseed with a couple of drummers playing Djembe as the sky became surely lighter in the East.

I lay on the ground there with them, wholly surprised to still be in my body, even to be back here on Earth after such a wild ride. Far out had a new connotation, and I had found the other side. Lighting his pipe, Andrew looked at me close in that pre-dawn light. A knowing grin and quizzical eye, he was clearly astounded by the journey we'd just made. So many lone wolfs, we had made the crossing together. He knew. He was there! Looking at me, I saw in his eyes and mind both an affirmation and a look of true wonder. Wild beyond imagination, who'd believe it?! Easy journey to other planets indeed! Reaching beneath my hoodie I pulled out the Peruvian quartz star seed crystal that had been hanging over my heart. The electricity of the quartz and static of my hooded sweater lit it up like a firefly. And there was I, on that mountain in the green light of dawn. Dust and vapor, vapor and dust, a gift of vision was in my hands.

THE END

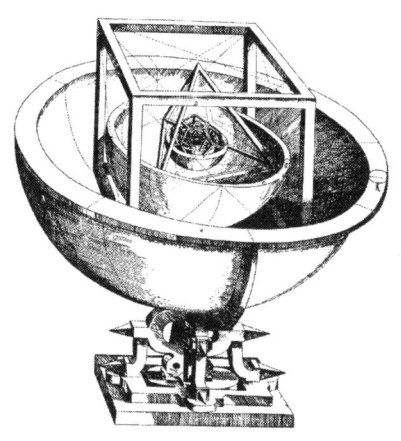

The Great Comet of 1996: Facts

Comet Hyakutake is a long-period comet. Before its most recent passage through the Solar System, its orbital period was about 17,000 years, but the gravitational perturbation of the giant planets has increased this period to 70,000 years. Cometary ices formed in different layers of the original interstellar gas and dust cloud that led to the solar nebula. The vast sphere of comets that surround the Solar System, called the Oort Cloud, may contain comets that formed from different solar nebula—that is, stars other than the Sun. Ethane was never before detected in comets or in interstellar matter, the ultimate source material from which the Solar System was formed. Comet investigators found levels of ethane in Comet Hyakutake that are about 1,000 times greater than can be explained if the molecules were formed by normal physical processes within the gases of the primordial solar nebula.

One theory is that ethane rich comets formed in the warmer region near the primitive Saturn and Jupiter, while those without it formed farther away from the young Sun, near the primitive Uranus and Neptune. Ethane and methane occur naturally on Earth and some other planets, and in certain meteorites, including the Murchison meteorite that fell on Australia in September 1969. While ethane is much less common than methane in the planets, it is almost equally abundant to methane in both Comet Hyakutake and in the Murchison meteorite.

April 23rd 1996. The Ulysses spacecraft crosses the comet's tail at a distance of more than 500 million kilometres (3.3 AU or 3×108 mi) from the nucleus, showing that Hyakutake had the longest tail known for a comet. The comet's tail is known to have been at least 570 million km (360 million miles; 3.8 AU) long. This is almost twice as long as the previous longest-known cometary tail, that of the Great Comet of 1843, which was 2.2 AU long. The solar wind had a velocity at the time of about 750 km/s (470 mi/s), at which speed it would have taken eight days for the tail to be carried out to where the spacecraft was situated at 3.73 AU, approximately 45 degrees out of the ecliptic plane.

Image Index

About the Author:

British/American artist, writer and consummate traveler, Paul Seftel explores themes and ideas revolving around alchemy, cosmology and energy. Born in London, England 1974, his paintings hang in residences, galleries and public spaces throughout the world. His controlled washes over horizontal canvases blossom with the natural drip and flow of colors and minerals, evoking metaphysical landscapes in the exploration of consciousness. Studio based in New York, you can see more of his work at www.PaulSeftel.com.

Printed in Great Britain
by Amazon